THE BLACK SLIDE

J.W. OCKER

HARPER

An Imprint of HarperCollinsPublishers

The Black Slide
Text copyright © 2022 by J. W. Ocker
All rights reserved. Manufactured in Lithuania.
No part of this book may be used or reproduced in any manner whatsoever
without written permission except in the case of brief quotations embodied
in critical articles and reviews. For information address HarperCollins
Children's Books, a division of HarperCollins Publishers, 195 Broadway,
New York, NY 10007.
www.harpercollinschildrens.com

Library of Congress Cataloging-in-Publication Data

Names: Ocker, J. W., author.
Title: The Black Slide / J. W. Ocker.
Description: First edition. | New York, NY : Harper, [2022] | Audience:
    Ages 8–12. | Audience: Grades 4–6. | Summary: Against his better
    judgment, fifth grader Griffin Birch follows his best friend down the
    new slide in the school playground, and at the other end of this portal
    they discover a cruel world populated by bloodthirsty creatures on a
    quest to become immortal.
Identifiers: LCCN 2021045325 | ISBN 9780062990556 (hardcover)
Subjects: CYAC: Resilience (Personality trait)—Fiction. | Survival—
    Fiction. | Horror stories. | LCGFT: Novels. | Horror fiction.
Classification: LCC PZ7.1.O1987 Bl 2022 | DDC [Fic]—dc23
LC record available at https://lccn.loc.gov/2021045325

Typography by Catherine Lee
22 23 24 25 26   SB   10 9 8 7 6 5 4 3 2 1
❖

First Edition

THE
BLACK
SLIDE

Also by J. W. Ocker:

The Smashed Man of Dread End

To Hazel Lenore, who took on the Black Slide
and escaped with only a broken foot

The Playground was an immense iron industry
whose sole products were pain, sadism, and sorrow.
—*The Playground*, Ray Bradbury

CHAPTER 1

It Didn't Look Safe

The Black Slide appeared on the playground of Osshua Elementary on a clear day in late September. Griffin Birch was the first to see it. His desk was near the back window of the Torture Chamber, so he had the best view of the playground. And that was too bad.

The Torture Chamber was the nickname of the fifth-grade classroom. Or one of the fifth-grade classrooms. Osshua Elementary had four, plus four third-grade classrooms, three second-grade classrooms, five first-grade classrooms, and two kindergartens. But only one classroom in the entire school had a nickname. A new fifth grader wouldn't find that nickname printed on the door or written in rainbow markers on the whiteboard—no, it would be whispered to them by another student at a lunch table or at the back of a school bus.

1

The Torture Chamber was the only classroom in the entire school with a view of the playground. Students had to sit and do math and learn grammar and take tests while the freedom and joy of that outside world tempted and distracted them. It was worse during recess for the younger grades. The fifth graders in the Torture Chamber had to watch other kids running and screaming and sliding and swinging and spinning and climbing while they sat and did math and learned grammar and took tests. It was, as the name suggests, torture.

Griffin had been thinking about his dad when he noticed the new slide. He was often thinking about his dad, who had been gone for six months. The first six months of forever, Griffin hoped. But he felt bad for hoping that. And he felt sad for his mom.

"Griffin Birch, eyes on your quiz or I'll stick you to the whiteboard."

Griffin jumped, tearing his gaze from the Black Slide to the white paper on his brown desk. Mrs. Pitts was a tall woman. She had other features, but tall was what you noticed when you saw her. Especially when she loomed over your desk. She was also mean, like she took the nickname of the classroom seriously.

She reminded Griffin of West Quoddy Head Lighthouse, especially when she wore red and white and the lenses of her large glasses caught the light and hid her eyes. He'd seen the red-and-white-striped lighthouse during a family vacation to Maine two years before. Despite its name, it stood at the easternmost point in the United States. He had clambered out on the rocks beyond the lighthouse while the Atlantic threw great nets of spray at him, salting his lips and dampening his hair. His dad yelled to him that nobody was farther east in the entire world than Griffin at that exact moment. Griffin knew he meant country, though. That was one of the few good memories of his dad that he had. And even then, his dad had tried to peg him with a half-filled soda can from the shore. His dad was also mean.

"Every year I want to cover those windows," said Mrs. Pitts. "But every year Principal Simmons says I can't. She says students need sunlight to grow. You know what I say to that, Griffin Birch?" She lowered her eyes behind her glasses enough to catch him in her lighthouse beam. "I tell her I can grow mushrooms."

Laila Davis turned slightly from her desk in front of Griffin's to give him a quick *be careful* look with the side of her face that Griffin could read as easily as if it were printed on the back of her shirt.

"There's a new slide," said Griffin. And that made Mrs. Pitts's lamp swivel to the windows along with the head of every student in the Torture Chamber. Even Laila's, and she never got in trouble for staring out the window.

The slide was a tube slide, the kind you jumped in at the top, disappeared for a few moments, and then flew out the bottom like a soda can from a vending machine. But it didn't look like a normal tube slide. First, it was black. Not sky blue or sunshine yellow or grass green. Just black. It also appeared to be made of leather instead of plastic, dull and textured like an elephant's hide, and it was fastened by large metal rivets. It seemed too tall, like the top was higher than the school building, but that couldn't be right. And it dove at an unusually steep angle to the red mulch that covered the playground. It wasn't anything like the gentle slide it had replaced. That one had been flat and orange. This new one reminded Griffin of a giant tarantula leg.

Mrs. Pitts walked to a window and stared at the empty playground with the sudden black tube slide in the middle of it. "They're always updating the playground equipment. Making it safer. Always new rules so that you kids can play without so much as skinning a knee. When I was your age, everything on the playground was made of metal that burned you on hot days, and towered tall enough to break limbs when you fell and sharp enough to cut skin so deep it needed stitches. It's either a wonder my generation lived

4

through childhood or a wonder you have a childhood."

Griffin stared at the Black Slide. It didn't look safe.

Mrs. Pitts sterned up her face and said, "Five minutes till pencils down. I'm expecting a lot of Fs on this one." Pencils were immediately pulled from teeth and behind ears and off desks and set to scraping across paper.

Griffin's pencil stayed atop his quiz, as lifeless as a fallen branch, while he continued to stare out the window at the Black Slide. It seemed to make the air around it murky.

Mrs. Pitts was wrong about why he stared at the playground. He didn't long to be out there. The playground had always terrified him. Made his stomach burn. His skin prickle. As far as he was concerned, that scary Black Slide fit the playground better than the happy orange one it had replaced.

He got a D minus on the quiz.

Mrs. Pitts docked him half a grade for doodling a long black tube at the bottom of the quiz with, for some reason, a small figure beside it.

CHAPTER 2

Dares Are for Dummies

Griffin's neck bent back painfully for a face full of blue sky before whiplashing to the ground for a face full of red mulch. He hadn't heard Ozzie Aldridge sneak up behind him. Had barely felt Ozzie's hands push against his shoulder blades. The sting on his palms told him he'd shaved skin in his fall, but what really hurt was his kneecap, which he'd banged bad enough that he grabbed it to his chest and rolled onto his back with a grunt.

"You gotta watch your back, Griffin." Ozzie had a way of using Griffin's name like it was an insult. Something about how he emphasized the *fin* part. Griffin saw Ozzie standing above him, heard him laughing with three voices somehow. Then Griffin saw Crystal Harp and Desda Perkins laughing behind Ozzie, the two girls close enough to each other they could have shared a backpack. Griffin

6

didn't think those girls ever got more than two feet from each other, like they were two heads of the same monster. They always laughed at him or made ugly faces at him if he accidently made eye contact. It was almost worse than Ozzie's sneak attacks.

But it all only happened on the playground.

Inside the school building, Ozzie and Crystal and Desda seemed kept at bay by the presence of teachers, the pressures of tests and essays, the principal's office three classrooms away. They didn't even acknowledge him. Desda had handed out worksheets in science class yesterday and hadn't so much as crinkled her nose when she'd placed a worksheet on his desk. But on the playground, they were predators. The difference between a python in a pet store and a python in the wild.

Griffin spat wood chips out of his mouth and looked for Laila. He didn't see her.

"Griffin's eating mulch!" somebody yelled.

"He likes the taste," said Crystal, giggling out of both heads.

"Get up, Griffin," hissed Ozzie. "Can't let the teachers see you down there. They'll think I pushed you." He extended a hand. "You know I'm just playing around with you. That's what you do on a playground, right? Play around?"

Griffin ignored Ozzie's hand and stood up slowly, favoring his knee. That's when he saw Laila, burning across the playground from the kickball field, a fiery comet of rage, scorching the grass, the mulch, charring playground equipment as she passed. She pulled up fast in front of Ozzie, sudden and hot enough to make him flinch, even though she was almost a head shorter. "Did you push him?" she asked, the words evenly spaced to give Ozzie time to think carefully about his answer.

"I was just helping him up." He glanced at Crystal and Desda, hoping for backup. He got giggles. "He fell."

"I'm always falling," said Griffin, staring at his shoes.

Laila was Griffin's best friend, except *best friends* was a terrible way to describe them. Griffin and Laila had been born only three days apart, March 31 for Laila, April 3 for Griffin. They had lived next door to each other their whole lives, the thin width of two side lawns separating their bedroom windows. Neither had any brothers or sisters. They were friends and siblings and neighbors, all in one.

They knew things about each other that nobody else in the history of the world knew. Like only Griffin knew about the time Laila had cut her leg open jumping the fence at the public pool when they had tried to sneak in after hours, gaining an ugly scar on her thigh that she always had to hide from her parents. And only Laila knew that Griffin had peed his pants when a group of teenagers jumped from behind a tree wearing pillowcases on their heads while they were trick-or-treating last year.

"If I ever see you touch him . . . ," she started but didn't need to finish. Whether it was the fire in her eyes or the fact that she looked poised to headbutt him, Ozzie took a step back from Laila.

"I've got an idea," he said, turning to Griffin, who was finding it easier to stand both because his knee felt better and because Laila was beside him. "Let's make a deal, Griffin." Ozzie raised his hand like he was about to pat him on the back but stopped short with a small wave when he saw Laila glaring at him. "I won't push you from behind for the rest of fifth grade if you go down the new slide."

Griffin blinked quickly at Ozzie. Heard the giggles of Desda and Crystal. It wasn't just him. Everybody felt weird about that slide. Griffin had stared at it all day. He'd been staring at it when Ozzie had shoved him. Nobody had used it yet. Not any grade. Not any recess. Nobody was even going near it right now. The Black Slide was scary.

"I don't want to," said Griffin.

"Come on, I dare you," said Ozzie.

"Dares are for dummies," said Laila.

"It's just a slide," said Ozzie.

"It looks like a big cannon aimed at the sky," said Crystal. Griffin liked that image more than a tarantula leg.

"I haven't seen anybody use it all recess," said Desda.

"Nobody used the slide that was there before," said Laila. "Not in fifth grade, at least."

The playground was a tricky place for fifth graders, even those who didn't have to put up with the likes of Ozzie and Crystal and Desda. They didn't want to act like the younger grades, squealing on playground equipment made for babies, so they found other stuff to do on the playground, like kickball or tetherball or dodgeball. Or hanging out by the school wall. Sitting in the swings without swinging. Lying on the merry-go-round without spinning. Hanging out inside the skeletal hemisphere of the geodome like it was a clubhouse.

The small group stared at the Black Slide. Griffin could see by the way Laila squinted at the slide that she also felt it. There was something wrong about that slide. Something dangerous. But the thought of Laila being nervous about it, the same Laila who had just quit her kickball game to blaze across the playground to stand up for him, changed his mind. It was his turn to be brave. That, and it really was a good deal from Ozzie. Laila couldn't always protect Griffin.

"You can't shove me the rest of the year?" asked Griffin. Ozzie nodded, holding both his hands out and wiggling his fingers to show that he wasn't crossing them behind his back.

"I'll do it," said Griffin.

"Griffin," said Laila, lowering her head and looking at him through her eyelashes. "Dares . . . are . . . for . . . dummies."

Griffin gave her a weak smile and walked slowly toward the Black Slide. Past the merry-go-round. Past the seesaws. Past the monkey bars and the trio of spring riders shaped like horses. The Black Slide never seemed to change. It didn't get bigger the closer he got. It was always bigger.

Take away the bullying, take away that he was supposed to be too old for it and, deep down, Griffin liked the playground equipment. He liked a good swing, the kind where you pump your legs so hard it feels like the swing is going to wind around the crossbar, and then you jump out of the slingshot seat to defy gravity for a single beautiful moment before dropping to the ground hard enough to make your teeth clink. He liked a good spin, too, holding on to the handles of the merry-go-round until he was dizzy and the force felt like it would shoot him across the playground. He liked clambering all over the geodome like a gecko. He even liked the seesaws and monkey bars and spring riders. Of course, he wouldn't be caught dead doing any of that in front of his classmates, and had to focus on avoiding Ozzie and Crystal and Desda. But he still liked it. Besides, he was

11

bad at anything with *ball* on the end of the word. He had to bunt in kickball, was the first one hit in dodgeball, always got rope burns on his arms in tetherball.

But there was something bad about the Black Slide, and the closer he got to it the more his steps slowed, like he was wading through ankle-deep sand.

Soon the Black Slide towered above him, a dull black mountain that blotted the sky, the metal rivets like so many eyes staring at him. Somehow, Griffin was able to free his foot from the sand and place it on the shiny chrome of the ladder. He took a deep breath and started climbing. It took only a few seconds to ascend, which made sense—it was a playground slide. But somehow he'd thought it would take much longer. That his arms and legs would be aching by the end of the climb. That he would be afraid of falling off the ladder. That it would make him dizzy. But, no, a few rungs beneath him and he was quickly looking into the hungry maw of the Black Slide.

He peered into its throat but couldn't see the bottom. Just blackness. The shell of the slide was too dense to let any light inside. But it wasn't that long, and it didn't twist. He should have been able to see a circle of soft red mulch at the end, mulch that tasted like bitter spices, he knew from experience.

Griffin thought about Crystal's comment, that it looked

like a cannon pointed at the sky. He imagined jumping into the top of the slide only to be shot into the air to land with a thud and a crack of broken bones a thousand yards away.

He looked over the top of the slide, the rounded black surface like the back of an orca. He saw Laila and everyone else below him. They seemed far away. They shouldn't seem that far away. The slide could only have been about— well, he wasn't good at estimating feet or yards—but they should only be seconds away, as the body slides. But he felt like he was on the high dive above a pool. His sweaty hands slipped on the chrome handholds.

He could see everything from up here. Every piece of playground equipment. The flat roof of the school. All the teachers' cars in the parking lot. He felt close to the blue sky, like he could reach up and scoop a handful of it and fashion it into a wet blue ball. He heard the shouts and yells and screams of his classmates as if from a great distance, like the sound had to travel through thinner atmosphere to get to him. For a second, he heard those shouts of joy turn to screams of terror. Like he had been misinterpreting that sound his entire life. The playground changed for a second. Became ugly. The way his dad looked like a monster for a moment when he got mad. The world disappeared, the kids disappeared, and the playground equipment looked old and rusty and abandoned. But with one blink, it was back to being a well-maintained playground full of kids.

And then silence, the whoops and squeals of joy ripped from throats and stomped underfoot. Griffin realized that, just like he could see everything and everybody, everybody could see him. Every kid on the playground was looking at him, like he was on the roof of the school building instead of at the top of a slide. The tetherball wound itself around its pole with nobody touching it. A kickball rolled lonely into the grass with nobody chasing it. The chains on the swings were almost solid bars, for all they moved from the kids sitting in their rubber slings.

He certainly couldn't give up now. Chickening out in front of every fifth grader in the school would have been worse than putting up with surprise shoves from Ozzie for the rest of the year. And almost worse than disappointing Laila. Although maybe he'd already done that by accepting Ozzie's dare. Maybe she wanted him to come down. He couldn't read her face from there. He should be able to read her face from there.

He sat down and stuck his legs in the slide, a torpedo in a submarine tube, and gripped the top arc of the slide in his hands. The slide felt strange to touch. Made his hands tingle like blood was rushing into them after falling asleep.

He could do this. He could slide down the Black Slide.

Even with the darkness chewing at his sneakers, he could do it.

He knew slides. They weren't fast. They were purposefully made to go slow. One hand or the skin of your leg would be enough friction to stop you. Sometimes you'd let go on a slide and not move at all. Or only move a little. Then you had to awkwardly shimmy your way down like it wasn't even a slide. He could do this.

He let go of the top of the slide. He let go into the darkness.

CHAPTER 3

Soft Child

Griffin regretted letting go as soon as his fingers uncurled. It was like something grabbed him by the ankles and yanked him down the slide. He rolled onto his stomach, desperately tried to grab the bottom lip, but his fingers merely grazed the edge, another tingle shooting through them, and now he was sliding backward down the incline. The Black Slide gulped, and he was gone.

It was fast. Wind screamed in his ears, and he could feel the cold tickle of his hair blowing away from his scalp. His palms burned against the slide as he tried to slow his descent, but it felt like he was skinning them worse than his fall in the mulch had done. At that speed, he should have landed at the bottom before he even felt those sensations, before he was able to form any of those thoughts. The cold, loud wind. His bleeding palms. But he was still in the slide. Still plummeting down the chute.

The Black Slide was not this long. Not this long by a lot. And yet he kept sliding, kept plummeting.

And then he stopped sliding. And that was worse.

It was like the slide had shot him off the edge of a cliff. One second his stomach and legs and hands were pressed against the interior of the slide, his body a straight line, the darkness and the pressing walls claustrophobic, the friction almost shredding his clothes and wearing at his skin, and the next he was spinning through void. His body flipped sideways and tumbled like he was rolling down a hill. His arms and legs splayed but didn't so much as graze the walls of the slide. The Black Slide wasn't that wide—this shouldn't have been possible. He was in empty darkness, the wind still shrieking, the cold still aching. He screamed and recognized the sudden familiar sensation of nightmare. Of scenes not connecting. Of going from one terrible thing to another terrible thing. Of situations not making any sense.

He had to wake up. That was all. He squeezed his eyes open and shut in the darkness over and over again. Sometimes that worked when he was having a nightmare. Screamed as loud as he could. Sometimes that worked. He twisted his body back and forth, searching for the sensation of blankets and mattress. Sometimes that worked.

But none of it worked.

Griffin did not wake up.

He kept falling.

Through emptiness. Through blackness. Part of him was waiting to smash into the ground, like he had been pushed over a real cliff. Another part of him believed he was falling in the other direction, upward, being ejected out of the planet like maybe he really had been shot from a cannon. Or maybe he was floating, twisting uselessly in the air. It was all darkness and loud wind and awful cold to him.

It wouldn't end. It wouldn't end. Why wasn't it ending?

After a lifetime inside that darkness, where he grew up and grew old and had thoughts he would never forget for the rest of his life, it did eventually end. He felt a solid shock in his body, like he'd hit the thin part of a funnel and found himself back inside the terrifying tube of the Black Slide. Except he wasn't sliding. He was rattling. Bouncing between the walls. Tumbling head over heels, and then sideways, like he was in a cement mixer that wanted to make triply sure he was evenly mixed before it poured him out. The walls felt like hard, cold rock, and every bump hurt, especially when it was his knee that he had already banged up or his head, which he tried to protect by wrapping his arms around it. The pain was almost welcome

18

after the nothingness of the void. But it was the confusion and the terror and the unending darkness and the claustrophobia of it that was far worse than the bumps and bruises. Until it wasn't worse. Until one bump caused a sharp jab of pain in his arm that penetrated all the way inside him and up and down his body. His skeleton was ossified agony, and his hand went limp and dropped from protecting his head as he screamed and screamed and screamed, in pain and in panic through the suffocating blackness until he shot out the bottom of the tube, landing flat on his back, holding his arm and whimpering.

He opened his eyes, but stabbing light forced them shut again. He squinted them into narrow slits but saw nothing but sky. The wrong sky. It had been blue and empty when he'd entered the Black Slide, but now it was a roiling gray, with bulbous sections of clouds flashing with internal lightning. He closed his eyes and turned his head to vomit on the ground.

He kept his eyes closed while his stomach threatened to heave again and the pain in his arm almost overpowered his body. As he lay there, he heard a strange sound, like metal scraping, creaky and slow. It grew louder as it drew closer. And he heard footsteps crunching the playground mulch. When it stopped, he felt the coolness of a shadow over him and heard words he didn't expect. "Soft child . . ."

But it wasn't quite a voice. The words weren't carried on breath. It sounded like rocks grinding together and the tines of a metal fork dragged across a ceramic plate, the two sounds creating the high and low tones of a windless, lungless voice.

And then that form changed. This one felt familiar. He recognized it as Laila even before he heard the beautiful breath of her voice. And she wasn't saying *soft child*. She was saying his name, "Griffin, Griffin, Griffin! Are you okay?" The sky behind her head was so blue and bright it hurt his eyes all over again, and he could feel the bottom of the slide exhaling a cold breath.

CHAPTER 4

The Swing Set Was a Gallows

Griffin had seen his future. He had gazed beneath his skin and his blood and his meat. Saw the glowing white scaffolding of his bones. All that would be left of him one day. They didn't look like his bones. Bones don't look like anybody's bones. But he knew they were his because that's what the doctor said as he held up the crystal ball X-ray. The doctor showed him and his mom the black hair of a line angled across the long, parallel white bones of his forearm that matched up with the pain he was feeling in it. That black slash—mid-shaft nondisplaced fractures of the radius and ulna, the doctor called it—was what the Black Slide had done to him.

He must have hit his head and blacked out in the Black Slide. Dreamed all the terror and void. Nightmared it. But he remembered it so vividly, could still feel the cold and wind and bruise when he closed his eyes. Dreams always felt like somebody else's memories, and they dissolved quickly in real life. His Black Slide experience stuck to him like his most traumatic memories of his dad. Griffin didn't tell his mom about what he had felt in the Black Slide. Or the doctor. He'd want to scan Griffin's head for a concussion. To see if he'd rattled his brain too hard inside his dice-cup skull. Griffin had had one of those scans before and hated the experience. Besides, his head felt fine. Physically, at least. The Black Slide still troubled his brain.

But the cast was worse than the fracture. It started at his thumb and ended past the bend of his elbow, freezing his arm in place so that he could only move it at the shoulder. He'd have to learn to use his left hand more. But that wasn't the worst part. The doctor's office had only two colors of cast left—yellow and purple. The doctor let him choose, but yellow or purple wasn't a choice to Griffin. He liked greens and browns, the colors of lizards and snakes. Those were his colors. Earth tones, his mother called them. So he didn't make a choice, and the doctor chose a bright yellow cast. His dad would definitely have made fun of him for that. Fortunately, his sling was black and that hid it well enough.

So: a painful break, an immobilized arm, a yellow cast, and to top it all off, he didn't even get a single day off school for his injury.

Laila walked into his room with the brazenness of Laila, not even yelling up the stairs to make sure he was dressed first. They usually met out front to walk to the bus stop together, but Griffin was running late. Being one-armed slowed him down. Especially when it came to feeding his reptiles. Laila found him awkwardly slipping live crickets to his bearded dragon with his left hand. Fumbling freeze-dried mealworms to his geckos. Clumsily tossing tomatoes to the box turtle. It was also time to feed his garter snakes, but he decided to put that off. Laila didn't like that he had to feed them baby mice. They were called pinkies because they were furless and looked like little pink gummy bears. And the garter snakes devoured them like they *were* little pink gummy bears.

Every pet in Griffin's room was scaled and cold-blooded. His mom didn't like his "creatures," as she called them, but she still allowed him to have them. Maybe she thought it made up for his dad. Most kids would rather have a puppy or a parrot, but Griffin thought fur and feathers were gross. He liked the clean slickness of scales. When a dog sheds, its disgusting hair coats furniture and clothes, and it smells. When a snake sheds, you can frame it and hang it on the wall like a museum specimen or work of art. When Griffin got older, a bit longer in the forearm, he wanted to work in the reptile habitat of a zoo, and he wanted to care for something larger than garter snakes and box turtles. Like Galapagos tortoises that you could ride, and boa constrictors that could swallow a person whole, and especially with Komodo dragons. His favorite reptile. They looked like living dinosaurs. Meanwhile, in his personal reptile habitat, he was still working his way up to an iguana.

"Shouldn't that chameleon be yellow?" Laila asked him.

Griffin looked down at the green lizard sitting delicately on his bright yellow forearm. He shook his head. "That's not how chameleons work. They change color based on mood, not surroundings."

"Can I sign it?" asked Laila.

"Why would you sign my chameleon?"

"Your cast."

"Oh." He gently placed the lizard back in its terrarium. "Sure, I guess."

"You ever going to name any of these things?" she asked him, looking around at all the coils and claws and yellow eyes and slit pupils. Griffin shook his head. He didn't name his reptiles anymore. Laila unsheathed a black marker that was suspiciously ready in her pocket and started scribbling on his cast.

"No, don't . . . ," he started when he saw what she was writing. It was her first name, which was fine, but she followed it with three exclamation points because she knew how much he hated exclamation points. Now it seemed like his cast was shouting at him. And it would be shouting at him for six weeks until he got the thing cut off. "Thanks," he said, slipping his yellow arm into its black sling.

"Your arm is a bumblebee," said Laila.

"*Your* arm is a bumblebee," said Griffin, wrestling with his backpack. He waved her away when she tried to help him and then followed her outside.

"How did you sleep with that thing on?" she asked as they walked to the bus stop.

"Awful. Felt like it was somebody else's arm. Gave me a nightmare."

"I had a nightmare too!" she said as if they'd both seen the same YouTube video.

The bus roared past, a giant yellow monster eating kids on the side of the road, and they sped up to meet it, jumping into its mouth like pinkies into fanged jaws.

They grabbed their usual seats in the back and sat in silence for a while, the bus rumbling beneath them and making their noses itch, the slow dread of a new school day growing inside them. Finally, Laila asked, "What was your nightmare about? The slide?"

Griffin hadn't told her about what had happened in the Black Slide. Or what he thought had happened in the Black Slide. Wasn't sure how to. "No." He paused. "Sort of? It was about the playground." That wasn't unusual. He'd had plenty of nightmares about the playground. He was always getting pushed off the swings or the monkey bars or hiding frantically inside the geodome even though that was impossible. Anybody could see you in there. Sometimes he was being pushed by Ozzie. Or he was hiding from Desda or Crystal. A few times it had been his dad or Mrs. Pitts. This nightmare, though, was different. "The Black Slide was there, but it was in the background. And it was much bigger. Like the size of a mountain. I was on the swings. Except it stopped being swings. The swing set was a gallows. You know, like they hanged pirates and witches on? Instead of chains and rubber seats, it was ropes. I had a noose around my neck, and even though I couldn't see it, I knew I was standing on a trapdoor. And I kept waiting for it to open and after, like, forever, I heard a thunk, I felt my stomach drop, and I woke up with this stupid cast across my throat."

"Weird. My nightmare was about the playground, too," said Laila. "I was on the merry-go-round, though. On my back, spread out, with my wrists and ankles tied to the handles." She raised her arms up and out from her body, almost hitting the head of the kid in the seat in front of them. "I could see a gray sky full of lightning and the top of the Black Slide, as big as a mountain, like in your nightmare. I was terrified that the merry-go-round would start spinning and make me sick. But it didn't, and I felt relieved but then it started to stretch me, pulling my arms and legs in opposite directions, like one of those racks from a medieval dungeon. I felt myself pulled longer and longer, longer than should be possible, but no pain. Although I wanted to scream like there was pain. A loud pop woke me up. I was all sweaty with my arms raised under my pillow and my legs spread apart so that they stuck out the sides of the blanket."

"Weird."

"Yeah. Your accident really got to us, I guess."

"I guess." Griffin looked around to see if anyone was eavesdropping on their playground nightmares. Nobody seemed to be. The younger kids on the bus were doing their usual things, talking loudly or jumping up and down and laughing. The older kids, though, the fifth graders, they seemed abnormally quiet, all of them staring out the windows. He looked outside. The school had come into view, the red brick building dominated by the dark slash of the Black Slide. Even from this distance it seemed too big. He turned back to the kids, who continued to stare, silent and strange, like they were all thinking about their nightmares.

CHAPTER 5

This Is Your Only Warning

Sometimes you're at the top of the seesaw with a rush, legs dangling, high above it all, and sometimes you're at the bottom with a thud, your spine jarred, choking on dust. Yesterday was definitely a thud to the ground for Griffin. But as soon as he entered the Torture Chamber, it looked like it was his turn at the top.

Ozzie, Desda, and Crystal were all gone. Just empty desks. Like it was National Jerk Day, so they didn't have to come to school. Maybe this was the universe making it up to him for yesterday. If so, Griffin thought he'd gladly break his other arm if it meant another day away from those three.

But then he saw the Black Slide through the window, a massive dark smudge on the glass, a blank spot in a broken mirror. Never mind. He wasn't going through that again. The slide loomed on the playground, not as big as in his nightmare last night, or as long as in his nightmare yesterday, but still too big, still too long. He kept waiting for it to move for some reason, to unmoor itself from its shiny ladder and slink across the playground, a giant black caterpillar. Griffin stroked his cast like he was holding his bearded dragon on his arm.

"Griffin Birch!"

Griffin's head twisted so fast his eyeballs had to catch up. The terrible lighthouse gaze of Mrs. Pitts blinded him.

"This is your only warning. If I catch you staring out the window again, I'll stick you to the whiteboard."

So it definitely wasn't a national holiday for *all* jerks. "Yes, ma'am." Griffin pretended the top of his desk was the most interesting thing on the planet.

On any given day in the Torture Chamber, it was almost impossible to keep from staring out the windows, but now that the Black Slide was out there, it felt whatever was beyond impossible. And dangerous. Griffin had this strange fear that if he didn't look at it, it would sneak up on him and swallow him down again. But he managed it, focusing instead on the strange emptiness of the classroom. Ozzie, Desda, and Crystal weren't the only ones missing. There must be a flu going around.

Griffin was also distracted. He had to concentrate all day on learning how to do everything one-handed and opposite-handed. Writing, drawing, flipping through books, using the bathroom. At times it was so frustrating he wanted to smash his cast against a wall or throw a book across the room.

During recess, he sat as far from the Black Slide as he could, over by the kickball game, where he watched Laila dominate the other fifth graders. It felt great to not have to worry about Ozzie. At least for the moment. He knew Ozzie would get around his promise. He might not shove Griffin anymore, but he might trip him or smack him on the back of the head or something equally painful. Griffin should have made him promise not to touch him. And there was still nothing he could do about Desda and Crystal. Even his broken arm wouldn't stop them. But he didn't have to worry about any of that for this recess.

By the end of the day, Griffin was getting the hang of being one-handed. So when he saw a motion in the window, he gave in to the temptation to look outside. Someone had walked up to the Black Slide. Nick Bromley. He was a fifth grader, but not from the Torture Chamber. Nick always reminded Griffin of one of those gangly lizards that stood up on their hind legs to run across water—basilisks, they were called. Also Jesus Christ lizards. It was the way he flailed his arms when he ran, just like those lizards dashing miraculously across the surface of a stream.

But Nick couldn't run on water, and he shouldn't be on the playground right now. All the recesses were done for the day. Still, Nick was standing at the foot of the Black Slide, almost where Griffin had landed with his fractured arm. And he was talking to himself. Or maybe he was talking to the slide? To somebody behind the slide?

Then Nick climbed the ladder.

Griffin went rigid. Terror ran up his legs and chest and face like he was covered in small spiny lizards. Helplessness dropped through his stomach like a weight. He couldn't yell to get Nick to stop. Or to get anybody's attention in the classroom. It wouldn't have done any good. He could only sit in horror and watch Nick perch himself at the top of the Black Slide. Griffin felt the inevitable next moment like a choking haze in the room.

Nick disappeared inside. He was there and then he wasn't.

Griffin felt himself dropping into the darkness of the Black Slide with Nick. The tingling of his hands, the friction against his palms and cheeks, the void and the cold and the wind, the tumbling of his body until it broke. He waited for Nick to drop out the bottom. Remembered how it felt landing so hard in such brightness and the lungless voice that hurt his hears. Wondered how hurt Nick would be.

But Nick never came out the bottom of the Black Slide.

CHAPTER 6

Where Is Everybody?

"Griffin, you miss your father, right?"

Griffin had finished feeding his reptiles and was rushing to the front door to meet Laila for the school bus. His mom's question stopped him like a wall.

She was leaning on the sink in the kitchen, a bowl of cereal in one hand, a spoon in the other. She was dressed for the office. Gray suit. Pink shirt. A gold rope necklace. Matching earrings. She was almost always dressed for the office. Like she was afraid her boss would drop in on her at any moment.

As she leaned against the sink, holding the spoon so loosely he thought she was about to drop it, he saw that look in her eyes. Or the lack of look. Like she was viewing movies in her head, movies of the past, movies of possible futures. They were all sad movies.

32

"Yes," said Griffin quietly enough that he thought for sure she would ask him to repeat his answer.

"He wasn't that bad, was he?"

Now Griffin felt up against that wall. "I'm going to be late for the bus."

"Yes, we don't want that," she said, dropping the spoon in the sink, where it clattered against the inside of the metal basin. Griffin winced and sped out the front door before she could ask him another awkward question.

Laila was waiting for him outside. "You okay?" she asked.

"I mean, I have a broken arm," Griffin said, lifting the yellow cast in its black sling.

"No, I mean, you look . . . never mind." Laila was good at giving him space when he needed it.

The yellow monster pulled up, and they jumped inside. As Griffin squeezed down the aisle, he scanned the green seat humps. No Nick. Just like on the bus ride home yesterday. And Nick wasn't the only one. "Does the bus seem emptier than usual to you?" he asked Laila as they sat down.

The bus was emptier. As was the Torture Chamber.

Ozzie, Desda, and Crystal were still not back. And scattered around their empty desks were more empty desks. Almost half the class was gone.

Mrs. Pitts stomped in like she was trying to make the

33

classroom shake, sweeping her gaze back and forth across the students, luring ships to the rocks instead of leading ships away from them. Everyone snapped to attention, eyes facing the front, but focused on the whiteboard, not on the terror that was Mrs. Pitts. "History books!" she said as she pulled a textbook from a stack on her desk. She looked around to make sure history books were being brought out across the classroom. One wasn't.

"Griffin Birch. Did you leave your history book at home?"

"No, ma'am. But . . ."

"But? But? But, but, but?" Mrs. Pitts dared him to make an excuse.

"Where is everybody?" He gestured around the classroom with his good arm.

Mrs. Pitts' face softened in confusion. But just for a second. Her eyes quickly rekindled, and she squinted hard behind her lenses like she was trying to set him on fire. "Stop fooling around and pull out your history book."

"But everybody's gone," he said. He looked around for support from what was left of the class, but they all stayed focused on their books. Nobody wanted to be in the beams of Mrs. Pitts's glasses. Laila gave him the sideways-glance warning.

Again the brief softness to Mrs. Pitts's face, like the classroom around her was fuzzy. Again replaced by hardness. "Everybody's here," said Mrs. Pitts, motioning to the classroom and then setting her mouth like she double-dared him to disagree. "Pull out your history book and be quiet." Griffin reluctantly obeyed.

Mrs. Pitts started reading a chapter, but Griffin couldn't pay attention. Why was she pretending that everybody was here? More important, where was everybody? It was like they had all disappeared, like . . . like Nick. As soon as he thought of Nick's name, Griffin's gaze magnetized to the Black Slide. There was something wrong with that slide. He'd believed that before his broken arm. He believed it even more after his broken arm. It looked like the fractures in his bones, a diagonal black line slicing across the playground. If something weird was happening at school, then the Black Slide was certainly what would show up on the X-ray.

Griffin saw movement by the slide. Another fifth grader, Stella, he thought her name was. He didn't know her last name. She was out there by herself, climbing the ladder.

It was a recurring nightmare. Griffin felt his body go wobbly, his ears rush with blood. "The Black Slide!" he shouted, jumping up and pointing out the window. Beyond the tip of his finger, he watched Stella slip inside the slide and disappear.

"Griffin Birch, that's enough!" Mrs. Pitts closed the

history book in her hand with a thwack and drew herself to her full height, which seemed almost inches from the ceiling.

Griffin counted the time by the heartbeats banging against his ribs, waiting for Stella to reappear. But, like Nick, she never landed in the mulch on the other end.

"Get up here and stick yourself to the whiteboard," said Mrs. Pitts.

Griffin looked around desperately, hoping somebody else had seen Stella disappear into the slide, but nobody seemed to have. He started wrenching his desk out of the line and up the aisle. It was difficult to do with one arm, and Mrs. Pitts didn't try to help or get anyone else to help him. He eventually pushed and pulled it to the front of the class, up against the whiteboard so that all he could see was dull white and the ghosts of past math problems. He could feel what was left of the class staring at the back of his head.

From that point on, the school day continued like any other school day, except Griffin had to stare at a whiteout and be uncomfortably close to Mrs. Pitts. He couldn't see the Black Slide from where he was, but he sensed it. It felt like a throb in his bad arm. An ache in his head and knee. A shadow that extended through the window and across the Torture Chamber.

Finally, class ended, and Griffin moved his desk back and joined Laila on the walk to the bus. The hallway was less of a cacophony than it usually was after last bell. All the younger grades clogged the hallways in lines and bunches, but the fifth graders seemed sparse. And even more seats on the bus were empty than had been this morning.

As it pulled away from the school, Griffin got a good view of the Black Slide again. It looked like one of his garter snakes after a particularly satisfying pinkie.

CHAPTER 7

It's Eating Kids

Laila was the queen of the universe. She was surrounded by glowing stars and colorful planets. Comets with bright tails swooped around her. Galaxies spun above her head like a collection of diadems. She was adorned by asteroid belts and planetary rings. Rockets rose on blasts of fire at her feet.

Laila was way into space. And her bedroom showed it.

She had astronomy posters and constellation charts on her walls. Model rockets on her desk. Photos of famous astronauts and space scientists like Mae C. Jemison, Ronald McNair, and Katherine Johnson framed above her bed. Her comforter was an invasion of fiery rockets. She shared the room with three different telescopes that huddled together on their tripods like gangly animals in a corral, hoping to be let out at night. It was more a science

38

classroom than a bedroom.

But Laila didn't just love space. She wanted to go there. Especially Mars. The red planet was the red apple of her brown eyes.

Sometimes Griffin and Laila talked space. And sometimes they talked reptiles. And sometimes—and these were the most fun conversations of all—they talked about the possibility of reptilian life on other planets.

But this conversation wasn't fun. Griffin felt like he was floating in the space of Laila's bedroom like an untethered astronaut, not wanting to tell her what he needed to tell her but knowing he would have to, that he thought the Black Slide was eating the fifth graders of Osshua Elementary.

"I don't get it," said Laila. "Is there something going around? Why wouldn't Mrs. Pitts talk about it?"

"I don't think anybody's getting sick," said Griffin. He was on the floor staring into the red eye of a rubber ball painted to look like Jupiter. "Did you look into the other classrooms? The younger grades are all full."

"You're saying it's just the fifth graders who aren't showing up for school?"

"Yeah." Ten bounces of this tiny gas giant on the floor, and then I'll tell her, Griffin told himself. Ten bounces was a long time for a right-hander throwing the ball with his left hand. "And I have no idea about Mrs. Pitts. I never have any idea about Mrs. Pitts."

"Was it a cut day? They better not have had a cut day without telling me," said Laila. She stared into space for a minute. Actually, a poster of space on her wall. "Where could they have gone?"

The ten bounces went faster than Griffin expected. Ten more bounces and I'll tell her, he said to himself. But when he bounced the planet again, it got away from him, ricocheting around the room searching for a stable orbit until going rogue and getting lost in a pile of clothes beneath a poster of a black hole. It looked round and dark and hungry, like the top of the Black Slide. Griffin stared at it until he couldn't take it any longer. "I think I know what happened to them."

Laila looked at him like he was setting up a joke.

"I think . . ." It sounded so crazy that it was hard to say. Even to Laila. He kept his eyes on the black hole. "I think the Black Slide ate them."

"Griffin." She almost said his name the way Ozzie always said it. "What in the world are you talking about?"

"I haven't told you what happened when I slid down the Black Slide." *Slid down* was a ridiculous way to describe his experience.

"I saw how you came out the other end. I mean, I don't understand how you could mess up going down a playground slide, but—"

"No, it was more than the broken arm and the bruises." Griffin got off the floor and sat down on the bed beside Laila. "How long did it take me to go down that slide?"

"How long?"

"Yeah. How long."

"Three seconds. You got in, you flopped out. That's a weird question."

"It . . . gets weirder." Griffin took a deep breath. "What I'm going to tell you is . . ." He faltered, started over. "This thing I'm about to tell you, it's going to sound strange. Like, really strange. But I'm not joking. I'm being serious. More serious than I've ever been."

They'd spent their entire lives together. Laila could read his face better than he could use his words. "Go ahead," she said.

He nodded slowly. "I was in that slide for hours. Days. Months. I don't know how long. But it was a very long time."

"I don't understand."

"It was three seconds for you, but for me, inside, it was different. Like I went somewhere else when I entered the slide. But not really somewhere. A nowhere. Just rushing through darkness. Like I was in space." He pointed at the plastic glow-in-the-dark stars glued to Laila's purple ceiling. "Like I was in space for a lifetime."

41

"You got a concussion. That's what it sounds like happened."

"No, I don't have a concussion. I don't even think I blacked out. Or at least I don't think that anymore. Not after what I've seen since then." He adjusted his sling to hide the yellow of his cast. "Yesterday, I saw Nick Bromley at the slide. You know Nick?"

"The Jesus Christ lizard?"

"Yeah. I saw him through the window in the Torture Chamber. He was out there on the playground by himself, and he was . . . talking . . . to the Black Slide." Laila opened her mouth to say something, but Griffin raised a hand to stop her. "Save your 'That's crazy' until what I say next. After he had a conversation with it, he climbed the ladder, dropped inside, and never came out the other end." He dropped his hand. "Now you can say it."

"That's crazy."

"And then today, you know when I yelled about the Black Slide in class?"

"And got the whiteboard? I was there."

"I had just seen Stella—I don't remember her last name—but she was out there by herself, just like Nick . . ."

"Talking to the Black Slide?"

"When I saw her, she was already at the top of the ladder. She went in, and she also didn't come out. Not after three seconds. Not ever."

"You're telling me a very weird story."

"The Black Slide is worse than weird. It's bad. It's eating kids. The fifth graders, at least. That's why so many are missing. They're going into the Black Slide and not coming out."

"Like, they're going in on purpose?"

Griffin shrugged his shoulders.

"It didn't eat you," she said.

"I know. But it chewed me up for a very long time. I could easily have gotten lost in there, I think." He felt sick thinking about being stuck in that void forever, caught in the throat of the Black Slide, never coming out. He felt sick for Stella and Nick and every other fifth grader who was missing. Even Ozzie and Desda and Crystal.

"You've had a thing for that slide since they put it up. Are you sure you're not just letting your nightmares get to you?"

"Wait, you're right!" he said, jumping up. "The Black Slide was in both of our nightmares. That's proof. I bet you all the other kids had nightmares like that. We all sense there's something bad about it."

"Maybe," she said. Griffin could tell she was at least considering the idea. Otherwise she would be treating the conversation like one of their "What would a sentient snake from Neptune look like?" ones. Hypothetical and ludicrous. It was a ludicrous idea, Griffin knew. But he also knew that it made more sense to him than anything else. "So you're saying that the Black Slide has been living off a steady diet of fifth graders ever since it appeared. That somehow they're either being lured or forced into the slide, and then they don't come out again. Why hasn't anybody else noticed?"

"I don't know. You saw Mrs. Pitts. She's not seeing it."

"Or maybe she's in on it," said Laila. "I wouldn't put it past her to have a killer slide for a pet."

Griffin didn't even register the joke. "And the playground, that's not monitored all the time. And the Torture Chamber has the only view of it. And some kids could be coming back after the school day is over." Griffin shrugged his shoulders, his yellow cast peeking out of its black sling again. "All I know is that kids are missing, I've seen two of them disappear with my own eyes, and . . . what I experienced in that slide. I bet that tomorrow more fifth graders will be missing. If there's any of us left."

"So let's watch."

"Watch?"

"Yeah. Let's see what happens tomorrow. See if there are more empty desks. And keep our eyes on the Black Slide . . . without getting busted by Mrs. Pitts."

44

"What?" Griffin shook his head and jumped up from the bed. "No way. We can't go to school tomorrow. We're in danger." Griffin was mostly thinking of Laila being in danger. He didn't know why kids were entering the slide, but he didn't want it to happen to her. Or himself, either, but he wasn't sure if the Black Slide would come back for seconds.

"You want us to fake sick?"

"Whatever it takes to not be at school with the slide." He looked down at his cast, which was almost all the way out of its sling. Laila's name yelled at him from it. "You don't believe me at all."

"You're telling me that our school has a carnivorous playground slide. That's going to take me a bit to process. Don't be mad at me." She smiled at him. "Do you still love reptiles? Do you dream about feeding hunks of meat to crocodiles?"

He sighed and then chuckled. It was a question she always asked him. And he had a response he always gave her. "Yes, I do. Do you still love the stars? Do you dream about making footprints on Mars?"

"I do. Now come on." She got up and helped him fix his sling. "If you really think we should stay home tomorrow, that's what we'll do."

Back in his own bedroom, full of scales instead of stars,

45

Griffin looked through his window and out at the dusk beyond the neighborhood. He imagined a giant mountain on the horizon, black and riveted. Hungry for kids. Ready to chew them up—or sometimes, to spit them out because it didn't like the taste of them.

CHAPTER 8

The Black Slide Will Eat You

Another night, another nightmare. The Black Slide was in it again, rising on the horizon, the defining feature of the landscape. Griffin sat on one end of the seesaw, high in the air, but backward, facing away from the down side. He heard that windless voice again, like silverware in a garbage disposal. "Soft child," it said behind him, making the skin on the back of his neck go cold. He heard screams. At first he thought they were typical playground screams, but they weren't. They were screams of suffering. He looked at his feet to avoid seeing the source of those screams. Below his sneakers he saw water, and in that water, his reflection, revealing him bound by rope to the seesaw. The water rushed up as the seesaw dropped to dunk him, and he awoke clammy in bed, his bad arm trapped behind his back.

Griffin didn't have to fake sick to stay home from school. His mom didn't wake him up or make sure he was on the bus. She used to, but not since his dad left. All he had to do was just not go to school. That easy. Still, instead of sleeping in, he got up at the usual time to feed his reptiles and turn on their heat lamps. They needed routine.

He dropped a quartered tomato into the turtle tank and looked out the open window. The morning seemed to be having trouble deciding on summer or fall. The sun was bright, and the trees green, but the air had a smoke and an edge to it. If fall didn't win today, it would win soon. The neighborhood itself was still, the only movement from a girl with a red backpack slung over one shoulder walking across her front yard.

"Laila!" he yelled.

She stopped and looked up. "What?" she yelled back.

"What are you doing?

"Going to school."

"I thought we were . . . but the . . ." He stopped yelling. No way was he going to shout about the Black Slide and skipping school across the entire neighborhood. "Wait for me." Griffin threw on his clothes as fast as he could with one arm and ran out after her.

Laila had stayed in the same spot but was looking down the road. "I'm going to miss the bus."

"I thought we agreed to stay home," said Griffin.

"I want to check out the Black Slide."

"No, you don't."

"Yeah, I do."

"It's dangerous. We talked about this."

"That's why I want to check it out. I'm allowed to change my mind." Laila was staring down the road. She hadn't looked at Griffin since he came out of his house.

"You were going without me," said Griffin.

She still wouldn't look at him.

A roar and a flash of yellow down the road. "I'm going to be late." She started walking.

Griffin grabbed the loose backpack strap. Laila jerked back like a dog at the end of a leash.

"Let go!" she said.

"No. You can't go near the Black Slide."

She slipped off the other strap, grabbed it in both hands, and set her heels in the ground. "Yes . . . I . . . can," she said, tugging at the backpack with each word. "Let go!"

It was tug-of-war. Griffin only had one hand, but it was twisted tightly into her backpack strap. She'd have to pull his arm from his socket to get the backpack away from him. "You're going to rip my bag!" said Laila, pulling harder despite her words. It was highly possible she could rip his arm from his socket.

"The Black Slide will eat you!" said Griffin.

"I dare it," said Laila. They started spinning as they pulled, and Griffin stumbled a bit. Having his arm slung to his chest hurt his balance. He had to be careful or he'd fall. But it wasn't his balance he should have worried about. Laila let go of her strap, and Griffin flew backward, hitting the grass hard enough that pain jolted through his bad arm.

"Why'd you do that?'" asked Griffin, wincing and holding his cast.

"You made me miss the bus."

"Good," said Griffin, trying to get up with one hand.

Laila watched him struggle to his feet by himself before shouting, "Mom!"

Twenty minutes later, Mrs. Davis dropped them both off at school with a wave. If Griffin couldn't stop Laila from going in, he was going in with her. Other than a few polite questions from Mrs. Davis about his arm and his mom, the car ride was completely silent. Laila didn't even turn around. Griffin couldn't figure out what was wrong with her. He kept analyzing yesterday's conversation in his mind, to see if he'd said anything to make her mad, but he couldn't think of anything.

Now he had to figure out how to keep her away from the Black Slide and also how to face Mrs. Pitts for not doing his homework last night. She was going to blast him into the sea.

50

As they walked to class, Laila kept looking at the playground. At the Black Slide. She did it enough that she bumped into him and caught one of her legs between his, sending him to the ground where he was barely able to break his fall with his good arm, although the pain that rattled it on hitting the asphalt scared him into imagining two yellow arms. "That's twice," said Griffin, staring nails at Laila.

"Sorry," she said, but kept looking at the playground. To see if anybody was talking to the slide, he guessed. Or getting eaten by it. The playground was empty.

And so was the Torture Chamber.

There was hardly anybody there. Mrs. Pitts sat at her desk looking dazed, like she was a substitute teacher covering a subject she had no clue about with students who spoke a different language. At first, anyway. As soon as class started, she was back to being the blazing lighthouse, although now that she had fewer points to aim her anger at, it burned hotter. She didn't acknowledge the skeleton class.

"Laila Davis! If you keep looking out that window, I will stick you to the whiteboard." Mrs. Pitts's glasses flashed.

Griffin couldn't believe it. Sure, he had been staring out the window himself, but Laila was usually careful. She never got in trouble. Laila shrugged Mrs. Pitts's reprimand

off. Didn't seem embarrassed by it. But she did stop looking out the window, at least.

Griffin didn't. He sagged down in his desk as far as he
could so that Laila's body hid him from Mrs. Pitts, and he
stared at the Black Slide. He was positive it was eating the
fifth graders of Osshua Elementary. He just had to wait for
it to happen, and then get Laila's attention when it did.

Mrs. Pitts's red-striped dress suddenly eclipsed his view
of the window. "Griffin Birch! Move your desk up front
right now."

He jumped and his face went red. He got up to drag
the desk one-handed to the whiteboard, but then asked,
"Can I just use one of the empty desks in the front row?"
He asked the question because it would be easier than
dragging his own desk up there, but he also wanted to see
if she would admit to the shrinking class.

"Stop fooling around and get your desk up there."

Apparently not.

He struggled with his desk and finally got it moving.
As he dragged it past Laila, he tried to make eye contact,
but she didn't look at him. She was gazing out the window.

A few minutes later, his vision a complete winter whiteout by the dry-erase board, he heard Laila's voice behind
him. "Mrs. Pitts, could I use the bathroom?"

Mrs. Pitts gave her the hall pass grudgingly. She didn't

believe any kid actually needed to use the bathroom during class, but she wasn't allowed to say no anymore. Not since that one kid peed his pants in her class last year. Laila took the laminated card and almost skipped out of the classroom.

Griffin didn't like Laila being away any more than Mrs. Pitts did. He kept his eyes on the door, skinks wriggling in his guts, waiting for her to return. He didn't get why she was acting so weird today. But he did know that it was extremely bad timing with the Black Slide lurking outside.

That thought made him turn in the other direction, to the front window of the classroom. He couldn't see the Black Slide from where he sat. Just the witch-dunking see-saws and the torture-rack merry-go-round.

He also saw Laila walk past, dropping the hall pass in the mulch.

He ran to the window.

Laila was talking to the Black Slide.

CHAPTER 9

What Happened to the School?

Griffin ran out of the classroom, banging his cast on Mrs. Pitts's desk as he passed, a pain he barely felt and a thump he barely heard over Mrs. Pitts's shouts for him to sit down. Some part of him wanted to obey her. To sit down and face the whiteboard and block everything out. Obeying was easy. Do what you're told and nobody yells at you. Nobody embarrasses you. Nobody makes fun of you. Nobody hurts you. Nobody notices you. It makes life easier.

But Griffin didn't need easier. Not this time. Griffin needed to save his best friend from a kid-eating slide.

If that were even possible. If any of this were even possible.

He tried to break into a run in the open hallway but could only kind of awkwardly hurry. He always found it awkward to run, but now he had an inflexible club of a right arm bouncing painfully against his chest. Still, he went as fast as he could, exiting the building and rounding the corner, terrified of what he would find—an empty playground with a Black Slide in the center of it all . . . that had just eaten Laila.

But Laila was still standing by the slide. Talking to herself, or it. Hope flared but was just as quickly doused. He knew what she would do next. She'd walk to the ladder, drop into the slide, and disappear forever. One more fifth grader gone and nothing he could do about it. No, not just one more fifth grader. Laila. He couldn't lose Laila.

"Laila!" He waited to feel Mrs. Pitts's hands on the back of his shirt, pulling him back to school.

But nobody stopped him. Which was great. But Laila didn't respond. Which was awful.

She kept talking, ignoring him like his reptiles did when he made faces at them through the glass of their terrariums.

"Laila!" he yelled again. But she kept talking to the slide.

He reached the playground, but his first step on the red mulch destroyed the world.

One step, he was on the grounds of Osshua Elementary. The sky was blue with gentle tufts of white. The air freshened by the pre-fall breeze. The buildings and parking lot and playground familiar. But then, like he had stomped on a switch, the skies changed to roiling gray with angry flashes of silent lightning burning the clouds. The air whipped into a chill that cut through his clothes and skin like he was being attacked by ghosts. The school disappeared. The parking lot disappeared. The world disappeared. There was nothing around but flat rocky desertscape as far as he could see. The only thing in the entire world was the rectangle of the playground that he stood on. But it had changed, too. All the equipment was warped and rusted and old. The chains on the swing set were bigger. The holes in the geodome tighter and more cage-like. The spring-rider horses snarled like predators on their coiled bases. It was the playground of his nightmare.

The only things that didn't change were Laila and the Black Slide.

"Laila, where are we? What happened to the school?"

Laila squinted at Griffin like she didn't recognize him. "Oh, hi, Griffin. I don't know. Maybe you should ask Gutter."

And in the silence, Griffin heard a scraping, like the creak of an old swing set or a squeaky seesaw pivot, but drawn out and warped—the same scraping he'd heard when he'd been ejected from the Black Slide.

And then something walked around the Black Slide to face him.

CHAPTER 10

You Would Hate the Painful Place

The creature Laila had called Gutter was the same height as Griffin, but thicker, wearing a long black robe with tight sleeves that was shiny like a raincoat and fastened with bits of metal. A shiny strip of the same black fabric dangled from its neck over the front of the robe. Its head was as white as pus and round like a stone that had been tumbled and polished but pulled out before it got too smooth. Instead of eyes, it had two metal spikes, like mirrored cones, jutting dangerously out of its face. Those eye-cones were what had made the scraping sound, as it dragged them across the surface of the Black Slide when it walked around it. Dragged its *eyes*. What was this thing? It didn't appear to have a nose or ears, and when it spoke, it revealed a small hole of liquid blackness framed by pointy metal teeth.

"You were supposed to come alone, soft child." The voice was the airless one he had heard after his Black Slide experience and in his nightmare. The rock grinding on rock. The metal shearing from metal. It made Griffin's heart shake and his teeth ache. There was no emotion in it, only sound.

"This is my friend Griffin. He must have followed me."

"Laila, what are you doing?" asked Griffin. "Who is this? What's going on?"

Gutter addressed him. "You should not be here. Only one at a time down the Black Slide."

The sky strobed with lightning, although the dark clouds stayed mute. The land, rocky and gray, stretched out too far and too empty in all directions, with the playground—or whatever it had become—the only thing in the entire wasteland. Griffin felt vulnerable and dizzy and couldn't catch his breath with all that space and air pressing down on him. He wanted to find his house and his room full of reptiles and crawl into bed.

He wondered if stepping off the playground would reset the world, drop him back into Osshua Elementary, but as terrified as he was of this place and the Black Slide and this Gutter creature, he was afraid that he wouldn't be able to take Laila with him. Maybe this was his only chance to rescue her, like she had done for him so many times with Ozzie and Desda and Crystal and even Mrs. Pitts. Maybe he could convince her to step off the playground with him. Maybe that would work. If it didn't, it was at least a step away from this thing, a step toward running away and finding help. If there was help in this desolate place.

"Laila, let's go."

She didn't respond. Just kept looking at the Black Slide like it was one of her beloved telescopes.

"Laila!"

"Leave the soft child be," said Gutter, its voice rattling Griffin's eardrums painfully.

"No, I . . ." It would have been a courageous sentence had he finished it, but he was interrupted when Gutter ran up to him fast, too fast, like time had sped up. Before Griffin could react, it had bent over and run its pointy eyes along his black sling, ripping the fabric and exposing the bright yellow cast with Laila's name on it. Gutter stood back up and opened its black mouth wide in either a smile or a snarl. The pointy metal teeth glinted wetly. "You opened the Black Slide." It pointed a pale, metal-tipped finger at him. "You do not need to visit the Painful Place."

"What?" Griffin didn't understand what the thing was saying. But that wasn't surprising. He didn't understand anything. He didn't understand where they were. He didn't understand what was happening. He didn't understand what was wrong with Laila.

Laila.

While Gutter had distracted him, she had walked over to the chrome ladder of the Black Slide.

He tried to run to her, to stop her from putting even a single foot on the ladder, but before he could take a step, he heard Gutter scream and, suddenly, both of his arms were caught in sharp vises.

Two more beings like Gutter had him pinned. They both had the rough, round vanilla-ice-cream-scoop heads and the conical eyes and the tight-sleeved shiny robes. But instead of being completely bald like Gutter, one had a metal mohawk of short spikes arcing over its head and the other had a ring of short, upturned spears on its head like a deadly crown.

Their fingers were like talons and they were breaking the skin of one arm and puncturing the cast on the other. Griffin tried to wriggle out but couldn't move. They were strong despite being kid-sized, their fists like stone and fingers like needles. One of them ground out words to him that he couldn't understand.

Laila was on the ladder.

Gutter spoke to Griffin. "It is too bad, soft child, that you don't need to enter the Black Slide. You would hate the Painful Place." It opened its mouth in a grimace-smile and spoke the word *hate* like somebody else might speak the word *love*.

Laila was at the top of the slide and was looking dreamily into its interior.

"Laila, don't!" shouted Griffin.

She looked at him for the first time since he had found her in this perversion of a playground. "It's just a slide," she said and then sat down to enter it.

CHAPTER 11

All by Themselves in the Dark Water

Fear. Pain. Helplessness. Griffin found himself reliving the Black Slide as he watched Laila get ready to jump into it. He couldn't let her go through that. And if she vanished like the other kids? No. He tensed, wanting to test how firm a grip the two creatures had on his arms, but he didn't dare. His only chance was to surprise them with a single desperate burst.

And it was desperate. He gave it all he had, twisting out of his torn sling, ripping his cast away from Mohawk Head, barely feeling the pain as his cast hit the creature in the side of the head with a solid thud, like he had hit a large rock instead of a flesh-covered skull. He used his momentum to yank his good arm away from Crown Head. He had freed himself for a moment, but that moment was all he needed. He made it to the slide in two leaps and tore up

62

the ladder one-handed faster than he'd ever climbed any ladder with two.

He heard an unintelligible rumble-shriek behind him and felt sharp claws in his leg, felt the pain and heard the ripping of fabric and was suddenly glad that ripping skin didn't have a sound. Griffin kicked at the small white, spiky boulder of a head that appeared below him on the ladder, the shock of its stony cranium traveling up his leg. But the kick seemed to land, because the creature fell from the ladder with a loud thump to the ground.

Griffin looked back up and saw that Laila had her legs inside the Black Slide. "Laila, stop!"

She pushed off with her hands, and he dove to grab one. He felt the fingers of his good hand tangle in one of hers, the heat of her palm against his own. She flew inside, and he went with her, jarring his cast on the bottom edge.

They were both in the Black Slide.

Griffin immediately steeled himself for what was to come, held on to Laila's hand as tight as he could for what she was about to experience for the first time.

But nothing happened.

Or at least what happened felt much different than before. It was like jumping into a hole. There was no slide around them, no shell of dull leather. But it wasn't like falling. It was gentler, maybe. Or quiet. He was still being knocked around slightly, but not hard enough that he feared losing hold of Laila's hand. Like minor turbulence on an airplane.

"Griffin?" Laila asked, her voice quiet and tiny in the darkness.

"I'm holding your hand."

"Are we in the Black Slide?"

"Yes."

"I'm sorry I didn't believe you. Is it going to get worse?" He could hear her fear. Could understand her fear. Felt her fear.

"I don't know. But this isn't what it was like my first time. I think we're going to be okay." He had no idea about that last statement, but he said it anyway.

"How did we get in here?"

"You don't remember?"

"I remember the school disappearing. And Gutter. But it's like I remember it through somebody else's eyes."

She had been controlled. Hypnotized. Pied Pipered. That explained how weird she'd been acting all day. The other kids must have been under the same spell. Except him, for some reason.

"Will you take my other hand, too?" she asked.

"I . . . can't," he said.

Laila actually laughed, and that made Griffin feel good.

"I forgot about your yellow arm. You should have asked for a glow-in-the-dark cast."

Griffin laughed, too.

The darkness whooshed by them. It could have been enjoyable, just the two of them, holding hands and sliding through the darkness, except for the uncertainty of what would happen next. If anything happened next. Griffin shoved that idea out of his mind. Even though it wasn't the chaos of his first descent down the Black Slide, this void was terrifying. "Do you still love the stars? Do you dream about making footprints on Mars?"

"Yes, I do," said Laila. "Do you still love reptiles? Do you dream about feeding hunks of meat to crocodiles?"

"I do. Tell me what the closest planet to our solar system is."

"Proxima Centauri b is the nearest exoplanet to ours. About 4.2 light-years away."

"How long would it take us to get there?"

Rushing darkness for a moment. "Probably six thousand years. Why?"

"Maybe that's where we're going now," he said.

"Maybe."

"Although I don't even like being on the bus for forty minutes," said Griffin. Laila laughed. "Have I ever told you about leatherback turtles?" he asked.

"No. But I'm imagining one of your box turtles wearing a motorcycle jacket."

It was Griffin's turn to laugh. "Close. They're sea turtles. Their shells are leathery instead of hard. They migrate every year across both the Atlantic and Pacific Oceans. One hundred and fifty thousand miles. A forever distance. And they travel it all by themselves in the dark water."

"Like us right now."

"Yeah." Silence for a long time, while they communicated only through the warmth of their clasped hands.

"When does this stop?" asked Laila finally.

"I don't know."

"Where are we going?"

"I don't know."

"What's going to happen to us?"

Griffin didn't have to fail at answering that question, too, because a jarring crash of knees impacting stomachs and heads hitting walls happened. They had reached the end of the Black Slide. It was a rough landing.

CHAPTER 12

This Must Be the Painful Place

The sensation of leaving the Black Slide felt exactly like dropping out of a regular slide, if that regular slide ended at a solid wall. Griffin and Laila let out a duet of escalating grunts as they slammed against hard surfaces and soft each others. Once everything was still, they realized they were stuck. They could barely move. And they were still in the dark. But at least they weren't flailing through void anymore.

"Are you okay?" asked Griffin, trying to remove Laila's elbow from his neck.

"I think so. Other than your cast poking me in the back."

"Sorry."

"Where are we?"

"I don't know."

"Why is it so cramped?" asked Laila, following it up quickly with "You don't know."

"Well, I don't," said Griffin. "And neither do you."

He moved his good hand across the smooth walls within his meager reach, at some point accidentally catching Laila's hair between his fingers.

"Ouch," she said.

"Sorry. I think we're in some kind of box." He kept his hand moving and quickly found an interruption in the smoothness. A square opening striped with bars. "Can you shift your body to the left?"

"I'll try."

"No, like, left."

"I am," said Laila.

"Oh, I meant right, I guess."

"Ouch. Watch it."

"Ouch back at you."

Griffin talked Laila through the game of Twister it took to wriggle into a position that freed him enough to wrap his hand around one of the bars and push his face against them, hoping he could see something through the window. He couldn't. It was as dark out there as inside the Black Slide. The air felt cold, but not like outside cold, more like an air conditioner had been turned up too high. It also smelled strange. Like the chemical smell a bathroom has after it's cleaned. He slowly squeezed his arm through the bars, half-afraid something out there was going to chop it off, and then a sudden rumble in the darkness caused him to yank it back, jamming his elbow into Laila's side. She yelped and tried to elbow him back but couldn't get the leverage.

"We're moving," said Griffin. This wasn't the smooth motion of falling through the Black Slide that they had just experienced. It was jerkier. Like machinery. The rumble grew louder and was joined by a piercing squeak above them as the small box they were trapped in started to vibrate and sway. It felt like going through the early stages of an amusement park ride, slow and bumpy and threatening a sudden drop.

Seconds later, the darkness thinned to a hazy dimness and the black box seemed to lower. They stuck their faces together at the window, partly to see out, but partly to relieve the growing claustrophobia that was threatening to panic them.

Above, among a labyrinth of black conduits, was a series of tracks from which hung boxes identical to their own—small, black, with a single barred window in one side. They couldn't see if any of these tiny cells were occupied, but they could see that they didn't sway or squeal like theirs did. The suspended cells moved steadily along the tracks like they were part of a factory assembly line.

Laila gasped. She was the first to look below.

They were inside a large building like a warehouse, the floor a good ten stories down. Thick white fog clung to the floor and billowed across it like drifts of dirty, shifting snow. Flares of bright red flashed here and there, staining the fog. They heard the ugly voices of Black Slide beings like Gutter echoing through the gargantuan space, cut through by terrifyingly human screams and shouts.

Where the fog thinned or when flares of light cut through it, they would catch glimpses of what was down there. Large metal devices spread across a vast metal floor. Black Slide beings—their white heads glowing like moons above their shiny black robes—working at the devices. And kids. Kids held captive in the devices or being led through the fog by the Black Slide beings.

It was like someone had taken the roof off a large Halloween haunted-house attraction so you could see everything going on at once through the strobe lights and fog-machine vapor. Every scary creature sneaking around. Every moment of terror and shock from the victims. They could hear the screams. Except these monsters were real, and those victims were real.

"What are they doing to them?" asked Griffin.

"I don't know," said Laila.

"This must be the Painful Place," said Griffin.

"The Painful Place?" asked Laila.

"Gutter mentioned it while you were . . . hypnotized." And Gutter had been right: he did hate it. Griffin tried not to focus on what was happening below as their cell moved across the ceiling, but that made him more aware of the squealing above them. "That noise is driving me crazy." Their cell began to swing ominously, and Griffin felt his stomach swing with it. "I don't think this cell was meant for two people." He said this to the back of Laila's head, which was currently pressed under his chin. Her hair smelled like honey and peppermint, and it was the only comforting sensation he had at the moment.

"There's something familiar about . . . down there," said Laila.

"Your nightmares must be worse than mine," said Griffin.

"Nightmares," said Laila.

The squealing above them increased to a torturous scream. Griffin squeezed his face against the bars to see what was happening. Bright sparks were flying from the connection of their cell to the track. "Uh-oh," he said. "I think we've broken this thing. It wasn't meant for both of us." He tried pushing on the walls to see if he could open a door, but nothing budged. Not that he had a plan if he had been able to open the cell.

"I don't want to fall," said Laila.

They weren't the only ones to notice. A cluster of the Black Slide beings had gathered around a bank of controls in the center of the room and were staring up at them.

The cell started to descend.

"They're coming to get us," said Laila.

CHAPTER 13

That Idiot Again

As they approached the large grid of black cells on the floor, their own cell started swinging more wildly, the overburdened connection throwing sparks like a fireworks show. Any second the cell would decouple from the track. They were in a race between landing and falling. Landing almost won.

A dozen feet from the floor, the box dropped straight down to the metal plating with a splash of fog and a squeal of metal, narrowly missing the nearest stationary cell. Griffin felt the impact in his teeth and broken bone, but fortunately, since he and Laila were packed so tightly in that cell meant for only one kid, they were cushioned from the impact.

As the cell hit, landing squarely and heavily on its bottom, the door flung open like it too was trying to escape the cell.

73

"They're going to be here fast. Let's go," said Laila, as if she were an expert at situations where you found yourself shooting through an eternal slide and shoved into a small box and dangled above haunted-house chambers full of beings with eye-cones and then dropped to the floor. Although as Griffin knew all too well, running away was a good bet in most situations, so he couldn't give her too much credit.

Even though the black cells on the floor were arranged in an orderly grid, there were still so many of them and they were packed close enough together that it felt like a twisty labyrinth. That plus the dimness of the building and the fog meant that a few steps out of the box, they were lost.

They heard rapid footsteps a few rows away and huddled behind a cell, hoping the Black Slide beings weren't headed in their direction. If they were, there was nowhere to hide, except inside cells. And Griffin didn't want to risk getting locked in one of those. He turned around, expecting a mob of boulder-headed creatures to boil through the fog behind them any second.

Instead, he saw a familiar face staring through the bars of a cell. Crystal.

She looked different without Desda, like a limb had been amputated. But she also looked bad. Like she hadn't brushed her hair or showered in a long time. Griffin whispered her name, and when she didn't respond, he elbowed Laila.

Laila's eyes widened and she stepped up to the bars and waved at the girl. But Crystal stared ahead like Laila was transparent. Griffin tried to figure out how to open the door, but it was a smooth, unbroken surface. He tried grabbing the bars and pulling, and then scrabbled his fingers across the surface of the door like it was a touch-screen. He walked around the entire cell twice, looking for a seam. There was no way to open it, short of dropping it from the ceiling. "Sorry," he mouthed to Crystal. She stared through him.

He felt Laila's elbow poking him. She held a finger in the air. He listened and heard the rock-and-metal voices of Black Slide beings.

Laila flicked her head, and they slipped away from Crystal, away from the voices. They passed other students, every one of them a classmate from Osshua Elementary. None of them seemed to register Laila and Griffin's presence.

A form moved slowly through the fog a few rows in front of them. They froze like tiny geckos beneath the shadow of a predator, hoping they wouldn't be spotted. The form was too tall and too thin to be a Black Slide being, and Griffin felt despair eat at his rib cage as he wondered what other nightmarish creatures prowled the Painful Place.

He felt lips at his ear and almost jumped straight back

up into the ceiling. Laila breathed a word to him, a word he didn't like. "Ozzie."

The fog parted enough to reveal the form behind it, but it took Griffin a few more seconds to recognize his least favorite person. Ozzie's hair was longer. He was thinner. Grungier. Listless. He had a loop of black material studded with metal around his neck. He didn't look like the monstrous kid who antagonized Griffin on the playground. He looked like what Griffin saw when Griffin looked in the mirror. Somebody cornered by a bully, without the hope of escape.

The loop around his neck was connected to a long black pole that came into view as Ozzie trudged forward. At the end of that pole was a Black Slide being.

It looked exactly like Gutter, down to the vertical strip dangling from its neck, except that this creature had a large triangle of metal bisecting its stony head, point-up.

Griffin turned to run.

Laila didn't. She charged.

Griffin could almost see the trail of fire behind her, not just a playground comet anymore, but a meteor. An asteroid. The fog swirled behind her as she threw herself at Triangle Head like she was ending the reign of the dinosaurs, smacking into it at full speed. Had that been Griffin on the receiving end of the asteroid, he would have fallen to the floor, all the air knocked out of him and maybe a rib broken. Triangle Head only stumbled a few steps and dropped the pole. But that was enough.

Ozzie might have looked downcast and weak, but as soon as he felt the tension of the loop around his neck loosen, he acted fast. He yanked it off and shouted, "This way!"

There were very few situations where Griffin would have run toward Ozzie instead of away from him, and this happened to be one of them. The three fifth graders zigzagged through the grid of cells as fast as they could, changing rows anytime they caught a glimpse of a white-and-black figure through the fog or heard the grating rasp of stone and metal.

Finally, they arrived at the edge of the cells, and Griffin realized where Ozzie was leading them—not away from everything, but to the middle of the space, the haunted house itself.

"Where are you taking us?" asked Laila. Too loudly, Griffin thought.

"I gotta get her," said Ozzie, and disappeared into the fog.

Griffin turned to Laila and shrugged, confused and helpless.

"I think we have to save that idiot *again*," said Laila.

CHAPTER 14

This Is Going to Hurt

Cold panic filled Griffin's limbs. "How?"

"I don't know. But not by running into those Black Sliders. It was like hitting a stack of rocks." Laila rubbed the side of her arm.

Of course Laila would come up with a catchier name for the creatures than he had. Griffin looked out across the white fog and flashing lights on the massive floor. It reminded him of a roller-skating birthday party that he and Laila had gone to when they were in fourth grade. The rink was a chaos of blinking colored lights and fog-machine vapor, and he'd refused to leave the wall at the edge of the rink for fear he'd get run over by some speeding roller skater. That's how he felt now. He didn't want to move from where he stood. The screams made him want to put his hands over his ears, and the thick white fog was a landscape of slow ghosts. He expected at any second a white head with pointed eyes and a small black mouth full of metal teeth would charge out at him. As the whiteness shifted and moved, it revealed Black Sliders running across the floor with those poles and Osshua Elementary fifth graders in those strange devices. But not too strange. Laila was right. They felt . . . familiar.

"I'm going after him," said Laila. And she did. The comet sliced through the fog fast and disappeared even faster.

What was he going to do? He wanted to follow her. Wanted her to take his hand and lead him. He wanted to just stay there and wait for her to come back and tell him what to do. But he couldn't. This wasn't the playground. He had to do something. It couldn't all be Ozzie and Laila knowing what to do. The whole thing felt like a video game—react, run, hide, time yourself, get ready for the next challenge.

And the one thing you don't do in video games is stay in one place for too long.

He remembered the bank of controls in the center of the floor. If he could get to the control center, and if enough of the Black Sliders were chasing Ozzie or out looking for him and Laila among the cells, maybe it was unattended. Maybe he could get there and add some chaos to this chaos. It was better than being scared of roller skaters.

Griffin sprinted across the floor, his cast smacking his

ribs with each stride. He wasn't very fast, and it was easy to get confused in the fog. A large bruise on his side later, Griffin saw the bank of controls raised on a short dais. It was empty. He leaped onto it. That was the hard part, he thought. Next was the easy part.

Except next turned into the impossible part.

The dais was circular, and around its edge was a series of thin curved stations for the Black Sliders to control whatever it was they controlled from here. Griffin had seen them use it to bring his cell down and hoped it controlled more than that. He was expecting buttons and levers and knobs and glowing screens. Anything he could mash or yank or hit or break and cause enough chaos in the workings of this place to distract the Black Sliders so that he, Laila, and Ozzie could escape. He had seen it work a thousand times in movies.

What he found was that each station was upholstered in an unbroken sheet of the same dull black leather that the Black Slide was made of. That's it. Like they were decorative, not functional. Like it was just a place the Black Sliders hung out instead of controlling the place. Where they set their coffee while directing the actions of the other Black Sliders as they took fifth graders from tiny black cells to scary devices. But he swore he'd seen them do something here to change the course of the broken cell he and Laila had arrived in. And this whole place had to be controlled somehow. There were lights and equipment and the ceiling tracks. But wherever those controls were, it wasn't here. He had finally jumped to action like Laila and Ozzie—and had failed. He had found the lounge, not the control center. So stupid.

A loud "Let's go!" from the fog shook him from his own fog as Laila flew past. Ozzie was right behind her, holding a girl by the wrist and almost dragging her along. It was Desda.

Griffin jumped in behind, just as two Black Sliders ascended the dais. He kept his focus on Desda's back as they all ran through the flashing red lights and white fog. Their feet clanged rhythmically on the metal floor, and sweat started to seep from his armpits. After what seemed like a marathon, they finally neared a wall and dove into a small opening.

On the other side of the opening was a small room, about the size of a bedroom. A chrome ladder like the one on the Black Slide was bolted to a wall and led all the way to the conduits and tracks in the ceiling. Another small opening across the room led who-knew-where. Everything led who-knew-where.

"Up there," said Desda. She spoke the two words flatly, like she was telling them which closet to hang their coats in. Griffin eyed the ladder uncertainly. It was a long way to the ceiling.

Ozzie prodded everybody else to go first, starting with Desda, and then Griffin and Laila. Climbing a ladder with one hand took timing and balance, and Griffin was afraid he'd run out of either one at any moment. He tried to hurry, but almost slipped off the shiny chrome more than once. It was even more pressure with Laila vulnerable directly beneath him. If he fell, he'd hurt them both.

Laila realized it, too. "Whoa, there. Take your time."

And then they ran out of time.

Griffin heard grumblings of stone and metal below and risked his focus on the ladder to look down. Three Black Sliders had run into the room. Fear filled him like a cold blush.

"Keep going!" shouted Ozzie. He had only ascended a few rungs, but instead of climbing faster, he dropped to the ground and ran off through the opposite door, abandoning the rest of them as easy targets on the ladder. Griffin looked up and saw that Desda was almost to the top. That meant Laila was the one most in danger right now. He tried to climb faster so that she could, too.

"They're gone," he heard Laila say below him.

"What?" Griffin looked around. The small room was empty again.

"Ozzie led them away." Laila's tone was one of disbelief.

Griffin shared it. "That doesn't sound like Ozzie. Why

didn't they chase us, too? We're sitting ducks on this ladder. Or climbing ones, I guess."

"They don't like it up here," said Desda from above.

"How do you know?" Griffin asked, concentrating on the rung directly at his eye level as he resumed his climb.

"I lived up here for a while."

She didn't explain further, and Griffin was having a hard enough time with the ladder to question the nonsensical statement.

Finally, they reached the top and found themselves on a platform among the ceiling guts, with all the scaffolding and tracks and platforms and conduits that they had first explored in their cramped, broken cell.

"Are you sure they won't follow us?" Laila asked.

"Pretty sure." Desda looked as dirty and bedraggled as Ozzie.

"How did they catch you, then?" asked Griffin.

"I came back down." No other explanation.

"So how do we help Ozzie?" Griffin couldn't believe that question had just come out of his mouth.

"For the third time," said Laila.

"We don't need to," said Desda. She was gazing around the dimness of the ceiling guts, like she was wondering where the furniture would go when she moved in.

"Uh, yes, we do," said Laila.

A sudden flare of anger and frustration distorted

Desda's face. "This is dumb. Ozzie should have left me down there. The Merciless will let us go when they're finished. And there's nowhere to run, anyway."

"The Merciless?" Griffin asked. "That's what they're called?" He had just gotten used to calling them the Black Sliders.

"That doesn't sound like the name of creatures that will let us go," said Laila.

That was a good point, thought Griffin.

Desda's face settled back into slackness, her eyelids drooping and her voice flattening. "I was like you when I first arrived in the Painful Place. I even managed to escape. I found a ladder and got myself lost up here like a rat in an attic." She peeked over the edge of the platform at the ladder, like she was gauging an escape route. "I couldn't find a way out of this place. Not a . . . good way. And I couldn't find food. And I was always in danger of falling. There was nowhere to go. It was terrible. But I spent a lot of time observing the Merciless. I watched them work."

Griffin shivered at the deadpan way she said *work*. "What do they do to the kids? What did they do to you?" asked Griffin.

"They hurt us."

"I don't want to get hurt," said Griffin.

"It's some kind of experiment. You have to get through

it to go home."

"I want to go home," said Griffin.

"What did you mean when you said—" started Laila, but she was interrupted by a heavy thud. They looked over and saw one of those beings Desda called the Merciless. It was on a platform across from the one they were on, the two of which were connected by a thin black metal beam.

"I thought they didn't come up here," said Griffin with difficulty, as every bit of moisture in his mouth and throat had flash-evaporated out of fear. He almost sounded like one of the Merciless. Desda shrugged and wrinkled her lips like it didn't matter whether she was wrong or right.

The Merciless walked out onto the beam unsteadily, as if gravity were pulling harder on it than it was on them. As it neared, Griffin could see that it had a web of chains wrapped around its spherical head.

Chain Head reached into its robe and pulled out a metal disc the size of its palm and with holes along one edge. It held the device flat in its hand, like it was offering it to them, its metal-tipped fingers inserted into the holes. The disc hummed with crunchy feedback like when microphones are too close together.

"This is going to hurt," said Desda, as if she were giving them directions to the bathroom.

CHAPTER 15

What Have They Done to You?

In his life, Griffin had experienced a wide arrange of emotions at seeing Ozzie. Terror when their eyes met on the playground. Rage when he passed him in class like they had never even met. Helplessness when he was on the ground looking up at him. Desperation at trying to figure out how to avoid him.

This moment, with a Merciless holding a weapon in its hand high above a hard metal floor full of fog-enshrouded terrors, he felt a new one. Absolute joy.

Ozzie popped out of some scaffolding and ran full speed across the metal beam as if it were as wide as a soccer field. He put both his hands out and gave the Merciless one of his trademark shoves in the shoulder blades.

When Ozzie did that to Griffin, Griffin always let out a grunt or a yelp or a shout. This time, Ozzie was the one who cried out, the shock of hitting the squat, solid creature jarring both his arms and jamming his shoulders, almost pushing him backward off the beam. Chain Head didn't so much as spit a rock of sound. It just fell off the beam, ricocheted off a length of track, and fell a hundred feet to the floor, where its head smashed into chunky white powder as the fog fled from the force of the drop. The sound was a small smack from this height, but it was sickening.

Ozzie joined them on the platform, rubbing his arms. He shrugged at Griffin. "I never said I wouldn't shove anybody else, Griffin." He put the emphasis on the *fin* part.

"We should move before another one of those things finds us," said Laila.

"It's no use," said Desda.

"You've become a real downer since the last time I saw you, Desda," said Laila.

"It's not her fault," said Ozzie.

"How are we getting out of here?" asked Griffin, who was trying to see in every direction at once, waiting for the next Merciless to come scrambling toward them through the ceiling guts. Desda's *This is going to hurt* echoed in his head.

The four stared at each other, not sure what to say or do or who should lead. Desda knew the area best, but it seemed like she was rooting for the Merciless. Ozzie seemed more concerned with Desda than with hiding. Laila was at a rare but understandable loss. And Griffin was Griffin.

Although Griffin at least knew the video-game rule. "Anything's better than standing still," he said quietly.

His statement seemed to shake Laila out of her paralysis. "Desda, do you know how to get out of here? Out of this Painful Place?"

"It doesn't matter," said Desda.

"That's great!" said Laila with false enthusiasm. "Then it doesn't matter if you take us there."

Desda opened her mouth to say something but shrugged instead. "It's going to be hard. Hope Griffin can make it." She nodded at him. He picked at his cast and hoped he could, too. She led the way, which was unfortunately over the beam. Griffin snuck a look down as he walked and saw the fog slowly swallowing the tiny form of Chain Head, lifeless and powdery.

Desda led them upward, deeper into the guts of the ceiling, and then back above the foggy floor. They clambered up ladders and down scaffolding. Across beams and tracks. Through tunnels and up chimney-like shafts. It was extremely slow going, and Griffin felt like he was in an obstacle course. Every once in a while, Desda would put her hand on a section of track to make sure no cells were coming. A few times they had to squeeze against the side of a tunnel as a series of them rattled past. Griffin made sure not to look into the barred windows as they went by him. He didn't want to make eye contact with anybody trapped inside.

It was hard doing the obstacle course with only one arm, but Laila helped him. She seemed distracted, though. Anytime there was a view of the haunted-house roller rink, she stared down there like she was daring herself to see what was happening. Griffin, on the other hand, couldn't look down, both out of terror at what was happening down there and at how high above the floor they were. And then there were the awful noises. The screams, the throat-ripping sounds of the Merciless. Now he could also pick up the faint buzzy feedback noise that Chain Head's disc had made. It was usually accompanied by a red flash.

Finally they took a break, hiding inside a large dark box perforated with short slits. They were sweaty and tired and bruised. It was warmer up here than in the coolness below. Griffin couldn't believe how big this building was. They all collapsed on the floor or against the walls except for Laila, who peered through the slits.

"How far across it are we?" asked Griffin, lying against a wall and breathing heavily. She didn't answer him. "Laila?"

She turned, the slits making faint stripes of light across

her face. "Griffin, that's our playground down there."

"What?" He rushed to the slits to look out. He thought she meant she could somehow see home. But that was ridiculous. It took him a while to see what she really meant. The white fog took its time shifting and thinning. It revealed the various devices and then hid them again like a cup-and-dice game. From what Griffin could see, the devices were bigger and more complex, but they did sort of look like playground equipment. Twisted versions of playground equipment, at least. Not rusted and medieval like in his nightmares, but sleek and strange like they belonged on an alien starship. And the layout was definitely Osshua Elementary's playground, just more spaced out across the massive floor. Over there was the swing set, larger than at home, and instead of swings, long tendrils of metal hung down from the cross bar. The merry-go-round was a wide, flat, circular table covered in straps for holding down victims. A hemisphere enclosure was the geodome. The Merciless were leading kids into it. There were also terrifying versions of the monkey bars. The seesaws. The climbing wall. The slide. A tetherball pole from which dangled a set of chains ending in metal spheres. Griffin was glad the spring riders were hidden by fog. He didn't want to know what they were here.

And while it seemed to be based on a playground, their

playground, this place definitely wasn't a playground. It was a painground.

"I think that's how this place is connected to Osshua," said Ozzie, who was lying on his back in the middle of the box. "Sort of like how walkie-talkies far away from each other can communicate by being tuned to the same frequency." He stopped his explanation. "Wait. How long have you guys been here?"

Griffin shrugged. "I don't know. A couple hours?" Laila shrugged and nodded her head.

"How long do you think we've been here?" asked Ozzie.

"You disappeared a little over two days ago."

Ozzie laughed, an ugly little sound that wasn't supposed to acknowledge anything as funny. "I've been here for months. Desda's been here even longer. She went down the Black Slide before me."

"What?" asked Laila half a second before Griffin said it.

"Look at us. Do we look like we've been here a couple of days? Time is faster here than back home. Although it doesn't feel faster."

By the dim light through the slits in the box, Griffin could see Ozzie staring wide-eyed at the ceiling. He felt sorry for the bully. "What have they done to you?" he asked.

"Awful things. Always in those devices. Strapped in or trapped in." Griffin could see Ozzie's eyes glisten.

"Do you know why?"

"They're experimenting on us," said Desda.

"What do you mean, experimenting?" asked Laila.

"They're looking for something. I'm not sure what, but they're using us to find it."

"That's awful."

"No, it's great." Desda sounded like she had reached the end of her statement, but Griffin and Laila weren't letting her off the hook. They stared at her until she explained. Desda huffed, but then continued. "Once they're done experimenting, they'll let us go home. They tell everyone that at the beginning."

"You really trust these Merciless, huh?" said Griffin.

"I don't," said Laila, nodding to the slits. "A lot of evidence down there against it."

"Whatever," said Desda. "We need to keep going. The faster I show you the exit, the faster this entire thing is done with." She stood up and left the box. The other three had no choice but to follow her.

Eventually, after more climbing, more clambering, more crawling, after more near misses with black cells trundling along their tracks, Desda stopped. They had just climbed down a long ladder to a ledge. They heard the buzzing feedback noise and saw a red glow below them. Desda pointed over the edge. They weren't above the painground anymore. And they were only a few stories up. They saw a small room with one of those thin black tables like the ones Griffin had mistaken for control panels. The table was beside a wide doorway the size of a garage door. But instead of a door, the doorway was filled by bright red light. Like the door was made out of red energy. Strangely, it reminded Griffin of home. His own front door was red, although a darker shade. It was also, of course, made of wood.

"That's the way home?" whispered Laila. Griffin could hear the careful excitement in her voice. He strained to see through the red light but couldn't see anything beyond it.

"No," said Desda. Griffin's disappointment turned sharply in his stomach. "The only way home is if they send you back after they're done experimenting. This is just an exit for the building."

"Good enough for me," said Laila. "I want out of this place." She shifted her body to climb down the ladder, but Ozzie shot out a hand to stop her.

"Wait a minute."

Laila stopped.

A Merciless walked into the room. It had a circle of sharp spikes radiating from its head like a halo. It approached the doorway, paused, and then stepped into the red energy.

Immediately, it bent over, grabbing its head, and shrieked metal and stone. It drowned out the noise of the red energy, and everybody except for Desda covered their ears, although Griffin had trouble doing that with only one arm. He tried to lift the cast higher, but that sent a sharp pain through his arm. He had to shove his right ear against Laila's shoulder. It didn't do much. He could hear the unending screams of the creature, and while Griffin couldn't see its face from his vantage, he could imagine the terrifying rictus one of those beings would show with their small black mouths and metal teeth.

None of the other Merciless entered the room to save Halo Head, and Griffin only wanted that to happen to stop that soul-bleed of a shriek. Knowing that thing down there was in agony made Griffin ache. He could feel hot tears on his cheeks, and his jaw hurt from clenching it. After a few seconds or a few minutes or a few hours, Halo Head stopped screaming, stumbled out of the glowing red doorway, and was gone.

"That's what you have to go through to get out of here," said Desda. Her cheeks were dry. "You have to suffer. The Merciless do it every day."

CHAPTER 16

They Like Pain

"It's called the Glare," said Desda.

"There must be a way to turn it off," said Griffin.

"Maybe," she said. "Maybe not. But I never saw it turned off the entire time I was in the ceiling."

"We should tell them about doors. Much easier to use," said Laila.

"They like pain," said Desda. "They like to hurt themselves."

"They like to hurt us," said Ozzie.

"Maybe. Or maybe they're indifferent to it. Maybe they think it's for our own good. But the faster we let them do it and get it over with, the faster we go home. You guys ready to go back now?" Griffin and the others stared at her in horror. "What else are you all going to do? Go through the Glare?" She nodded down at the red energy field filling the exit.

95

The girl was getting on Griffin's nerves. She sounded like an adult. Everything is practical and inevitable with adults. His dad was the worst about it, always saying things like "That's the way life is" and "Life isn't fair" and "You do what you have to do." But Desda, like his dad, wasn't completely wrong, either. Griffin thought of the pain of hitting the ground after Ozzie's shoves, the pain of the Black Slide that first time, of his fractured arm now. He didn't want pain. Maybe not even if it meant escape. Although it sounded like they only had two options, and both involved excruciating pain.

"What are we going to do?" asked Ozzie.

"We have to get out of here," said Laila, although the way she held her eyes, you could tell she was having a hard time imagining walking through the Glare. Griffin thought she was brave just for saying it out loud.

"Yeah, I don't know how bad I want that now," said Ozzie, gazing at the door and then looking at Desda.

"We have to do it," said Laila. Brave again.

Griffin knew he needed to be brave, too. "We need to at least try," he said, sort of hoping that the Merciless would catch them first.

"You guys realize we're made of different stuff than the Merciless," said Desda. "Our bodies probably can't take what theirs can."

96

"We need to at least try," repeated Laila, looking at Griffin. She stepped to the edge of the platform, waited to make sure none of the Merciless were near, and then dropped quickly down the ladder into the room. Griffin followed her, and after a few moments so did Ozzie and Desda.

They stood in front of the noisy Glare, and Griffin wondered again what that disc was that Chain Head had. It had sounded sort of like this Glare did. The red energy gave off no heat. They couldn't see through it to what was on the other side. Or maybe they could and there was nothing on the other side. Step through that and they could find themselves in the emptiness of the Black Slide again. The sinister glow reflected off their faces as they stood in an arc around the door, not sure what to do next, knowing exactly what to do next.

Griffin thought of Laila and said, "I'll go first. But I'm going to need help." He squinched his face and forced the next words out. "Ozzie, can you push me through it?"

"You want to me to shove you, Griffin?"

"*Want* is the wrong word."

"Not for me. I totally want to shove you. Just like old times."

"Whatever. Do it hard enough that I go through fast." Griffin looked over at Laila.

"It's not a bad idea," she said. "Except for whoever the last person is."

Dang it, thought Griffin. That meant going last was actually the brave move. He could never get it right.

"One hundred eighty seconds," said Desda.

"What?" asked the other three in staccato.

"That's how long you'll be stuck in the Glare. I counted it back when I was living in the ceiling. Back when I thought there was a chance of escaping."

"Three minutes," said Griffin. "I can do three minutes."

"Once you're in it, it's not up to you," said Desda. "You can't get out until it's over."

Griffin had never liked Desda, but he was finding new reasons here in the Painful Place to not like her even more. He stared at the Glare, taking deep breaths like he was about to dive into water, and then squared up to the glowing red field. He could almost feel pain just being this close to it. "Shove me," he said to Ozzie.

Griffin had barely gotten the *me* out when his head snapped back, he saw the intestinal black ceiling as a blur, and then he banged his chin on a cold, hard surface and his broken arm smashed against a solid wall. He dropped, dazed, and it took a few moments to hear quiet arguing above him. He ached like he'd walked through the Glare.

But he wasn't through the Glare. He was still in the Painful Place. On the floor of the Painful Place. "Did you miss? Did you shove me into the wall?" he asked Ozzie when his head cleared, but still not getting up from the cold metal floor.

"No way, square into the red. I'm good at shoving. You bounced off it like it was a cement trampoline."

"He didn't miss," said Laila.

"The Merciless pass through it voluntarily," said Desda. "And never in a hurry. They just step in. Maybe that's what you have to do."

"That might have been better to know thirty seconds ago," said Griffin, getting up slowly. He was in pain without even having been subjected to the Glare. He couldn't do it, could he? Just slowly walk into it on his own? He could barely tolerate the aftermath of hitting a regular old wall.

But then he saw Laila walk right into the Glare.

99

CHAPTER 17

We Are Very Far from Home

Laila's scream was loud and strange and unlike any sound Griffin had ever heard come out of her mouth. Her body twisted into a position he had never seen her take. It was like she was suddenly a person he had never met, or he was seeing a side of her she had never shown him. Like Laila's real self was agony. It made him sick and angry, and he moved to grab her and pull her out of the Glare, but Ozzie stopped him.

"One hundred eighty seconds," said Ozzie.

Griffin wished he were brave enough to punch Ozzie in the face and rescue Laila. But a stupid, smart part of his brain told him Ozzie was right. He had to let Laila hurt.

It felt longer than three minutes. Longer than three hours. He watched her writhe and scream and every once in a while her eyes would open and look in his direction, but he knew she wasn't seeing him. She wasn't seeing anybody or anything. Just reacting to the pain coursing through her, pain meant for beings of metal and stone and only to scare away beings of soft flesh and fragile bone.

Griffin's eyes teared, and it seemed like she was melting in the red glow, dissolving in pain, being worn away by suffering. But he blinked and he blinked and he held his breath and he didn't look away for even a moment, and soon enough Laila collapsed through to the other side. He could barely make out the outline of her form through the red, a crumpled lump on the ground outside.

Griffin didn't hesitate this time. Didn't ask for help. He walked right into the red Glare, his yellow cast held in front of his face like he was walking through a hard wind full of dust. His last sight before entering the redness was Laila's name shouting at him from the gaudiness of his cast. Three exclamation points.

And then it was nothing but torture. He tried to breathe, but he was inhaling an erupting volcano. He tried to run or drop to the ground, but he was in a paralysis of pain. Like he had a cast over his entire body and it was filled with biting and burning and slicing things. He was suffocating in boiling water while metal blades scraped his skin and then muscle and then bone away. He tried to count the one hundred eighty seconds, but it took an eternity to get to two. He was turned inside out. Smelled burning and blood. Heard his own screams like knives in his eardrums.

And then he felt the cool bliss of relief, as he fell to hard, cold ground, sweat soaking him and the Glare behind him. He felt the most mundane sensations of existence—the itch beneath his cast, the pressure of his tongue on the roof of his mouth, his eyeballs shifting in their sockets—and they all felt like grand exultancies of eternal joy. And then Laila was shouting at him, not from his cast, but from beside him on the ground. She smiled at him and hugged him, and he loved it, but he knew it wasn't a complete smile or a complete hug. That there was icy terror in her face and limbs, a slight contraction of the corners of her mouth and looseness of her arms, like too big of a smile was a lie, too hard of a hug was lie. And he knew because he felt it, too.

He looked back at the Glare, looked back at it like a past self, and could see the dim forms of Ozzie and Desda on the other side. They seemed to be arguing, but Griffin couldn't quite tell through the red. But he didn't care. He didn't feel the urgency that he'd felt on the other side of the red door. Wasn't panicked that the Merciless would catch them and lock them back into cells. He didn't even think he cared about being strapped to monstrous playground equipment. Nothing was worse than what he'd just gone through, and nothing was better than what he was experiencing right now.

Until a horror of a thought hit him.

If the Merciless caught him and Laila now, they would have to go back through the Glare. Griffin didn't want to go back through the Glare. Not ever again.

"Hurry up, Ozzie!" He didn't know if Ozzie could hear him or if he should be shouting, but he needed to say something. A few moments later Ozzie stepped into the Glare.

This time, Griffin watched with fascination as he sat on the ground, his arm loosely around Laila's shoulders. It wasn't like watching Laila being tortured by the Glare. He could be more objective with Ozzie, after all the pain and terror that Ozzie had caused him. Still, Ozzie did seem to have changed since he'd dared Griffin to enter the Black Slide. He still pronounced Griffin's name like it was an insult and he still had that glint in his eye that jabbed ice in Griffin's bones, but he seemed different. And if he'd been here as long as he said he had and if he'd gone through what he said he had, he probably was changed. But even if he was still the same cruel Ozzie, Griffin had learned he didn't want to see him in pain, didn't want to see him trapped in the Glare. Not Ozzie. Not Crystal or Desda. Not even Mrs. Pitts. Maybe his dad, though. Maybe his dad.

The three minutes finally passed, and Ozzie was out

and sweaty and breathing like he'd never had air in his lungs before and crumpled on the ground with Griffin and Laila. But he didn't hold on to the euphoria of exiting the Glare. He immediately looked back. "Desda?"

Griffin could just make her out. She'd been standing in front of the door while Ozzie was trapped in the Glare, but as soon as he was out, she turned and walked back in the direction they had come from—back, Griffin knew, to the tiny cells and the painground and the Merciless.

"She's not coming with us," Ozzie said. It was a statement of sudden realization. He looked destroyed, pained, like he was still in the Glare.

Griffin heaved himself up from the cool ground that, he noticed for the first time, was metal, as metal as the floors inside the building. He turned around to see where they were.

"We are very far from home," he said.

CHAPTER 18

Are They Afraid?

Griffin remembered sitting on the slimy, periwinkle-covered rocks past West Quoddy Head Lighthouse, being the farthest person east in the entire country. He felt so much farther away than that now. And had so much more to fear than his dad chucking soda cans.

It seemed to be nighttime outside the Painful Place, but it was a strange shade of night. The darkness of the sky wasn't a cozy blue-black pricked with stars. More like just thick, solid black, like a heavy bowl covering the world. No stars. No moon. But an eerie light stronger than a full moon illuminated the landscape and made sharp shadows scarier than if it had been pitch-black out. The source of light was large, glowing cloudlike forms in the sky. They weren't wispy or vaporous. They seemed thick, like irregular-shaped metal blimps somehow moving about the upturned bowl of the sky.

The light from the glowing metal clouds revealed massive fields of flat metal all the way to the horizon, riveted and plated like someone had fastened it to them, a desert of metal. Unlike the floor of the Painful Place, the land was completely clear of fog. Not a single tendril of it crept its way along the ground. Fang-like curves of black rock sprang from the metal land, which was tufted here and there by patches of short black grass and dotted with tall lumpy white mounds. They looked like those twenty-five-foot-tall termite mounds in far-off countries, but instead of being made of brown dirt, it was like they were made of frozen heaps of mashed potatoes.

In one direction, far away and hazy, the light-studded buildings of what must have been a city rose on the horizon. In another, the shards of strangely shaped mountains like so many giant black claws reared ugly into the dark sky, their sharp edges glinting dangerously in the cloud light.

"This is what Desda meant by no escape," said Ozzie, his shoulders slumped like he was about to melt into a puddle on the metal beneath him. "She was right."

Two clouds scraped against each other like buses passing too close in opposite directions, grinding their metal sides together with tooth-aching noises. The friction caused the clouds to glow brighter and spew a rain of large sparks onto the cold metal ground.

Griffin had the urge to rub warmth into his arms, but his cast prevented the action. It felt cold. Not like winter, but like the cold of autumn that feels refreshing at first, but then slowly burrows through your coat and sweater and shirt and skin and muscle and leisurely freezes your bones until suddenly you're cold deep in your marrow and can't get warm even if you come inside and tunnel under a blanket.

In the distance, from the direction of that menacing city, a fast-moving light headed toward them. "What's that?" asked Griffin.

"We need to hide," said Laila.

Griffin and Ozzie agreed with their feet, all three running along the side of the building they'd just left. It was bigger than any building that Griffin had ever seen. It must hold much more than just the painground.

The unspoken idea was to run around to the back of the building, but it was quickly obvious that it would take too long to get there. Fortunately, there were smaller satellite buildings scattered around. They were black and odd-looking, built into shapes that Griffin's elementary-school geometry hadn't prepared him for.

They flattened their backs behind one that looked like a cube and a cone had been smashed together. The light was getting closer, but Griffin wasn't looking at it. His eyes and mouth opened larger, and he placed a trembling hand on Laila's shoulder, squeaking out a quiet sound of shock and terror.

Laila looked up. "Oh no," she said.

Even this far from the Painful Place, they still couldn't quite see the true size of the building. But they could see above it. From its roof slanted a long black antenna, a black tether streaking the sky diagonally. It looked like a black straw sticking into the Painful Place, but Griffin knew what it really was.

It was the Black Slide, and it extended high up into the sky past the light of the glowing clouds to disappear into the blackness beyond.

"It's so big," said Laila, which was a phrase Griffin had heard her use before, many times, but always when she was looking up at a sky full of stars.

The only reason Griffin was able to tear his eyes from the Black Slide was because staring up that high made him dizzy. He focused on the metal bolts and seams at his feet until the vertigo ended and then shifted his gaze to the approaching light.

It grew larger, elongating into a long black snake of a train. It was sleek and silent and had no windows or doors that he could see. The only feature was the cyclopean light at its tip. The train stopped in front of the Painful Place without a noise, and two dozen Merciless exited out of small holes that suddenly appeared in the side of it. They walked steadily toward the front of the building and the Glare, which was a dim flicker of red that far away.

"I don't want to hear this," said Laila. Griffin and Ozzie both nodded and started making their way through the maze of buildings like they had made their way through the maze of cells minutes before. Or hours. Had it been days? Griffin thought. It couldn't have been days. He would be hungry and tired if it had been days. And he was only tired. Sticking close to the cool sides of the Advanced Geometry buildings, they finally made it around the Painful Place, and they managed to do so without hearing a single Merciless scream.

The landscape at the rear of the building was similar to the front. Another complex of small black buildings surrounded them. More mountains on the horizon. The only difference was that no city loomed in the distance back here.

"Our only way home is through the Merciless," said Ozzie. "Desda was right. We have to go back. It's our only option."

"No way," said Griffin. "I'm not going through the Glare again. Not back into one of those cells. Not onto their painground."

"Sometimes you have to make a tough choice," said

Ozzie. Griffin wanted to punch him again.

"You've been here for a while," said Laila. "You really want to go back after all the experimenting they did on you?" Ozzie didn't answer, and Laila turned to Griffin. "Painground? Did you make that up?"

Griffin shrugged. Or tried to. Halfway through, his shoulders by his ears, it turned into a shiver. "They found us," he said, turning slowly.

They were surrounded by about fifteen Merciless. The small stone beings were spaced irregularly throughout the complex, like they were all looking for the best places to hide for a game of hide-and-seek. Laila went with a different metaphor.

"This is the worst surprise party I've ever been to."

Griffin, Laila, and Ozzie looked at each other for half a second, and then they ran out into the flat metal wilderness.

Ozzie took the lead with his long legs, but Laila wasn't too far behind him. Griffin would lose to both of them on a good day, but his cast really slowed him down. When his lungs were at the burning point, he had to concentrate on breathing and running and not jolting his cast too much and fighting the urge to look behind him, and he ended up tripping over a small bit of black grass that the darkness had hid. Well, it looked like grass, but *grass* was a horrible term for the stuff. When he sat back up after jarring his skeleton on the metal ground, his pants were sliced even more than when the Merciless on the playground had ripped them, and a dark rivulet of blood oozed down his leg. The grass was as sharp and stiff as sword blades. He looked up in a panic, remembering that this particular danger was a lesser one than what they were running from.

But the Merciless weren't following. They were in their same places, the party frozen midsurprise, the hide-and-seek game abandoned. They still seemed to be staring at the three, but they weren't following.

"Guys . . . guys, wait!" yelled Griffin. Ozzie and Laila pulled up near one of the lumpy mashed-potato piles.

Laila ran back to him and, after looking at his cut and dubbing it a "Band-Aid scratch," helped him up and over to the mound. Up close it was as tall as a house and about half as wide. Its surface was smooth and bumpy, like it had been polished. He leaned back against the mound. It was hard, like plastic, and cold. Everything felt hard and cold here. "Why aren't they following us?" asked Griffin.

"Yeah, they could have picked you off easily," said Ozzie. Maybe Griffin didn't need to punch him in the face. Maybe an arm cast to the back of the head would be more satisfying.

"Knock it off, Ozzie," said Laila. "This is the same

feeling I got in the Painful Place." They all looked back at the black building. They couldn't help it. Griffin tried to follow the Black Slide with his eyes, but its far end disappeared into the darkness where the light of the clouds couldn't reach. "Other than that one that followed us into the ceiling guts, the Merciless didn't seem too eager to capture us in there. As many as there were, we shouldn't have been able to escape—" She bit off the end of the sentence, but Griffin knew what she had almost said: *that easily.* The Glare hadn't been easy. It had been degrees beyond hard on a scale probably not explored by any human being before.

"Desda said it didn't matter," said Ozzie. "Maybe they know that we have to come back. That our only path is back."

"Maybe Desda's crazy," said Griffin.

"Don't make fun of her. I'll shove you right into that black grass," said Ozzie.

They watched as the Merciless turned and shuffled away, like they were bored by the kids. Then they were just gone.

"Are they afraid?" asked Griffin.

"I don't think they're afraid of anything," said Ozzie. "They use pain lasers for front doors."

"Shhhh!" Laila hissed. Griffin and Ozzie turned to look at her. "Do you hear that?"

Griffin strained his ears in the strangely lit darkness. He did hear it. Faintly. It sounded like metal grazing metal, the *shrik-shrik-shrik* of a classroom full of scissors during arts and crafts, snipping away. Goose bumps boiled the skin on his arms and neck. He had no clue what would make a sound like that here.

"Where's it coming from?" asked Ozzie.

"It sounds like it's all around us," said Laila. She stood up from where she leaned against the mashed-potato mound. "It's getting louder."

"Closer," said Ozzie.

Suddenly, the noises were joined by vibrations. They felt them through the metal ground and the mashed-potato mound.

"Something's coming," said Griffin.

"I think it's already here," said Laila.

CHAPTER 19

Stick Your Arm in Its Mouth

The tall white mound that they had just been leaning on juddered and shifted. They all moved away quickly, thinking it was about to collapse. It did worse than that. It broke apart into five creatures. Each was three times as tall as Griffin on its four thin metal legs. They looked like lumpy white hermit crabs, but with no head, and their legs were jointed like a spider's. They sounded like scissor blades when they moved, and each leg ended in a sharp point.

As always, running seemed to be an appropriate response, and then an absolutely necessary one as the creatures immediately started chasing after them. One of the creatures scuttled directly over Griffin, giving him an unwelcome view of its underside, which all metal teeth and glistening black mouth. All it had to do was bend its legs and it could snap him up in two bites. Maybe three.

But he supposed he wouldn't feel anything after the first one, so the final count didn't matter.

Griffin sped up so that his view was back to cloudy black sky instead of sharp teeth. There was no cover nearby, nothing he could do to help Laila and Ozzie. Nothing they could do to help him. Just animal danger and animal instinct and animal survival. The creature caught back up to him easily and squatted so that its toothy maw lowered closer to his head. Griffin dropped to the ground, but the thing kept lowering. He tried to kick at one of the thin legs, but it seemed bolted to the ground. Griffin threw his cast over his head and felt a painful crunch vibrate through his arm as the thing bit the cast. He rose into the air, dangling from its jaws by his injured arm. He screamed, and he could hear echoing screams from Ozzie and Laila. Familiar screams of their own pain and terror and doom. They were being eaten alive as surely as he was being eaten alive.

As the horrible chewing continued above him, he wished the creature's mouth were bigger so that it could eat him in one bite and get it over with. He couldn't stand to listen to his friends in pain for one more second.

Wait.

Their screams sounded different now. Not pain and doom and terror anymore. It wasn't screaming. It was shouting. Ozzie and Laila were shouting at him.

They were yelling to him. Something about his arm.

He turned his head as he dangled from the metal teeth of the creature and saw Laila and Ozzie standing beside each other. They were each holding one of their arms as they shouted. He finally made out what they were saying.

"Stick your arm in its mouth!" shouted Laila.

"What do you think it's eating?" he yelled back. Not only was he going to be devoured by a monster in a strange world far away from home, he had to have an argument while it was happening.

"Your other arm," shouted Laila. "Stick your good arm in its mouth!"

That sounded crazy. But right now everything was crazy. The Painful Place. The Merciless. Hanging with Ozzie. Hanging from this creature like he was a piece of tough meat caught between its teeth. Any second it would make its way through the cast and cut through his thin arm and then the thin bone he knew was under there now thanks to the doctor's X-ray, like it really had been a crystal ball telling his future, telling him this was the bone that the monster would eat first when he died.

And now his friends wanted him to stick his other arm inside that dark hole lined with metal teeth, the more vulnerable arm that didn't even have the protection of a cast sheathing it. Crazy.

But then he realized that they had somehow survived the attack and weren't dangling from a mouth. And he'd already survived the Black Slide and the Glare, so why not? Why not stick both of his arms inside the creature's mouth? He jabbed his other arm up, timing it with the rhythm of the creature's chewing that was as familiar to him now as his own heartbeat, so that both arms were above his head like an inverted high diver. Its metal spikes dug into his arm and he screamed in pain and instantly regretted every line of thought that had just flossed his brain and everything Laila had said to him and he hated Ozzie for the millionth time in his life, and then suddenly he wasn't dangling anymore, he was falling down to the flat metal ground. He landed with a thud and decided that nothing in the world made sense, so he was going to lie there and pray for unconsciousness and nightmares.

CHAPTER 20

Why Aren't We Dead?

The next form looming over Griffin wasn't another hungry mouth of metal teeth, but Laila. He flashed back to the Black Slide, falling out of it and hitting mulch. Laila had been there for him then, too. And when he'd fallen through the Glare, she'd been there on the ground waiting for him. And every time Ozzie had shoved him, she had been there to help him. This time, it was Ozzie and Laila helping him up together. And he never thought he'd miss playground mulch so much.

Ozzie and Laila looked awful, all ripped sleeves and dripping blood, like they had tried to donate blood to a psychotic nurse at a Red Cross drive. He looked down at himself and knew that if they looked awful, he looked awful with about fifty more aw's in it. His cast was a mess, his sleeves were shredded, his pants ripped, and he was covered in both dry and wet blood like it was part of the outfit he'd chosen for the day. The blood seemed darker in the surreal cloud light.

"Why aren't we dead?" he asked, less as a sincere question and more as a half-hearted regret.

"I don't know, but as soon as they bit down, they dropped me and Laila," said Ozzie.

"We must taste bad," said Laila.

"Maybe we're poisonous," said Ozzie, looking at the lacerations on his arm like he had a new appreciation for the limb. "Which could come in handy, other than the fact that they have to chew us a bit to find out. Either way, your cast stopped you from being tasted. If it had grabbed your other arm, it would have been a shorter ride for you."

Griffin looked at his mummified arm. The yellow fiberglass had been punctured and cracked, and the under-sleeve was torn and frayed. Somehow, the cast was still doing its job of keeping his arm immobile. Barely. If his arm weren't hurting, he'd be tempted to rip the whole thing off. And of course, somehow Laila's name had survived and still shouted at him for attention.

"You're into animals, right, Griffin?" asked Ozzie. "What do you think of those frozen mashed-potato monsters?"

"Reptiles. I'm into reptiles. And those creatures are . . .

more cold-blooded than reptiles, if they even have blood in them." Griffin looked over at the creatures. They had assembled themselves back into that tall, innocent-seeming white mound to wait for more palatable victims. "At least we know to avoid them now." He had leaned so casually on that mound just five minutes before.

"Avoid them on the way to what?" asked Laila.

"Good question." Griffin gazed across the metal landscape. In the distance, he saw a flash of light on the bleakness of the horizon, like the first stretch of a sunrise. For a second, he experienced joy at a darkness about to be relieved. But it wasn't dawn. He didn't know what it was. It seemed to be a large chunk of crystal floating on a rainbow of colors. But then it disappeared, like it was an illusion of distance and atmosphere. The only thing left on the horizon was an indistinct mass barely lighter than the darkness around it.

"Should we try that hazy area?" said Griffin.

"Why?" asked Ozzie.

"Because we've got jagged mountains over there, mound monsters here, the Painful Place and a city full of even more Merciless somewhere behind us. By process of elimination, we might as well try the haze. Unless you've got a better idea."

"I might." Ozzie's eyes strayed back the way they had

come, where they could still see the massive black building topped by that angled tube that pierced the sky.

"No," said Laila.

"We're not going back," agreed Griffin.

"What?" Ozzie kicked at the metal ground like he was trying to scuff dirt and winced when he stubbed his toe. "You guys just got here. You're not the bosses. You don't know what to do."

"We're not telling you what to do," said Griffin. "We're telling you what we're going to do. Or I guess, what we're *not* going to do." Being assertive was difficult.

"Okay," said Ozzie, looking at the Painful Place. "Maybe I'll go back by myself."

"Do it," said Laila. "Go to that torture trap. I'm tired of rescuing you."

"Watch out for the frozen mashed-potato monsters," said Griffin.

Griffin and Laila walked toward the gray haze, which suddenly seemed much, much farther away than when Griffin had suggested it.

A fast patter of shoe rubber against metal rushed at them from behind, and Ozzie appeared beside them. "You're still not the bosses," he said.

Griffin was surprised to find he felt relieved that Ozzie was staying. He still didn't like the kid, but his dislike had lessened since they'd arrived at the Painful Place. But the real reason was that they had a better chance out here with three people, especially since one of them was one-armed.

They walked for what seemed like hours, the hard ground making Griffin's feet and legs ache. If he'd thought it would be more comfortable to sit or lie down on the unforgiving metal, he would have suggested it, but that sounded as horrible as walking on it. As they trudged along, they passed more mound monsters and more fields of spiky black grass, which they looped around in big serpentine coils. They passed what looked like impact craters, dents in the metal ground big enough that Griffin could almost have laid down in one. Sharp boulders like giant black stalactites jutted from the ground. The sides of the stones had wide facets like cut jewels. Griffin kept seeing the boulders as fangs and waited for the landscape to come alive and eat them with those black teeth.

The worst part was the insects. They were constantly besieged by tiny flying creatures whirring at their faces. They learned fast not to swat them, though, as the hard metal wings were razors that cut their faces and the palms of their hands. They had to shake their heads like horses and hope the creatures would go away.

"What the heck?" said Griffin, forgetting again that they weren't regular flies and gashing his hand trying to swat one out of the air. His fear was fighting with his anger for top emotion. "Is everything deadly here? I could live a week outdoors back home and not come across a single animal. This place is crazy. Like Australia." He'd heard that almost every plant, insect, and animal could kill you in Australia. He knew that the reptiles definitely could. They had some of the biggest crocodiles in the world and most of the world's deadliest snakes. Many of the lizards were venomous there, too. Griffin looked around the barren landscape of bright metal and black stone. He couldn't see the Painful Place behind them anymore, and the Black Slide was lost in the darkness of the sky, but he could still feel it behind them.

A loud shriek and flash of two clouds rubbing together broke him out of his anger and reverie. "Let's get to the haze," he said gruffly, and trudged faster across the riveted metal plain. Laila and Ozzie exchanged looks and followed. Eventually, the misty gray mass on the horizon hardened into dark stripes.

"Is that what passes for trees here?" asked Laila.

The haze was a forest. If Griffin squinted his eyes. If he had never seen a forest before. If he hated forests. The trunks of the trees were thick, straight metal poles. Clustered at the top of the poles, instead of boughs of soft green leaves, were hard metal cages. Each trunk bore about ten skeletal cubes, the sides of which were straight bars, topped and bottomed by sheets of metal, all clumped together in a lumpy mass. The cages were about the size of the cells in the Painful Place. Kid-sized.

A cold wind passed through the cage forest, and the bars of the metal boughs rang and scraped against each other like creepy wind chimes.

"What do we do?" asked Ozzie, who knew exactly what they should do but wanted to delay it with a question.

He didn't need to. Laila and Griffin had stopped already. The forest wasn't the type of place you just walked right in. It was the type of place you looked for any reason to not enter. Finally, after not finding one, after all the other places they could go seemed far worse, they walked into the metal woods. Into what should have been shelter from this strange, dark world and the Painful Place far behind them. But it didn't seem like shelter. They felt more vulnerable. The cage trees blocked most of the cloud light, plunging them into darkness, and what little filtered through the bars revealed an antiseptic woodland. No undergrowth, no fallen leaves, no rustling of small animals on the ground or flitting of birds in the trees. That ever-present forest energy was dead here, replaced by bare metal ground and unnaturally straight rows of pole-trunks topped by bundles of shifting cages.

124

The sound of the cages rubbing and clanging lightly together all around them was unnerving, and Griffin found himself staring up at the boughs thinking something had moved them. That it was more than the cold wind causing them to sway. Each pole was large enough to hide something or somebody behind it, and he eyed each one warily as they approached it.

Forests back home had their spooky side, but this one was spooky from all sides.

They walked in silence, like they were terrified of bringing attention to themselves. Something must call this place home. Something must hide here. Griffin was about to admit his mistake, to beg them to leave this place, to turn around and run back into the openness of the metal fields, where they could at least see danger from far away. Where the cloud light gave some relief from the suffocating darkness.

"This place is terrible," said Ozzie suddenly.

Griffin knew Ozzie was just trying to break the tension, but it was the most unnecessary statement Griffin had ever heard spoken in his life. When he turned to tell Ozzie that, he saw the boy pulling back his hand in a fist. "No, don't!" Griffin yelled, but it was too late. Ozzie punched the trunk of the nearest cage tree hard, and it sang like dull metal.

Ozzie froze in place at the sound, ignoring the stinging in his fist because he hadn't realized it would be so loud. Laila froze too. So did Griffin. They listened to the echo bounce among the pole-trunks, waiting for something to return the sound. To acknowledge the greeting. Or worse, to follow the sound. To step or creep or slither or jump out from behind a pole-trunk. To appear at the summons.

"Look out!" Laila screamed.

CHAPTER 21

The Black Slide Is the Only Escape

At Laila's frenzied warning, Griffin looked behind him to see what was coming, the Merciless or the mound monsters or whatever called the cage forest home. If he had been the one Laila was screaming at, he would have been eaten immediately. Fortunately, Ozzie looked in the right place, directly above him, where one of the cages was opening like a pair of metal jaws, the bars like long, thin teeth, reaching out to gobble him whole. He jumped back and it snapped at the air where he had been standing, and then retracted like an empty claw in one of those arcade gaming machines, sad and slow. They all backed away from it but found themselves backing into other cage trees, which extended their branch-necks and opened their cage-mouths to devour them.

They ran.

This wasn't a place they could hide. A place they could be even temporarily safe. A place where they could sit and figure out what to do next. This was yet another place to get eaten.

Their running seemed to stimulate more cage trees, and the soft scraping and tinkling that had been the eerie soundtrack to the forest became terrifying groans of metal and loud snaps of barred jaws.

Fortunately, because the rows of trees were so straight, they knew exactly how to retrace their steps out of the forest. Unfortunately, that put them equidistant from all the biting, snapping cage-jaws lining the way. One bar-tooth snagged Ozzie's shirt, ripping it and giving him two torn-up sleeves. Griffin almost tripped over Laila's foot, but the stumble saved him from getting swallowed into a cage. But through luck and desperation and terror, all three made it out of the cage forest, bursting into the open where no tree could reach them, the dark sky seeming slightly less oppressive, the cloud light slightly less creepy, the field of unending metal slightly less unwelcoming. But only temporarily.

Out of danger for the moment, Griffin screamed, in frustration instead of terror. "What are we supposed to do? We escaped the Merciless, we escaped the Glare, we escaped the mound monsters and—and—and . . . aaaauuuggh." He ran his good hand through his hair and walked in a circle before tromping over to a cluster of rock fangs. He sat down hard on the cold metal ground, careful not to brush against the sharp edges of the black rocks.

Laila was soon beside him on the ground, and Griffin looked at her in a panic. "Why is everything trying to hurt us?"

"I told you we should have stayed where we were," said Ozzie, rubbing a finger over the flat parts of one of the rocks like he was playing a game of chicken, waiting to draw blood on one of the edges. "I think we've proved that there's no other way out. We need to go back, face the Merciless, and hope they finish with us fast."

"You keep saying that. Finish what? Why are they even doing this to us? To our class? What are they looking for? Why are they experimenting on us?" It looked like Griffin was yelling at Ozzie, but he was really yelling at everything in the entire metal and rock world around them.

Ozzie opened his mouth to answer, but then shut it for a few seconds before saying, "I don't know."

"It's a nightmare. Nightmares don't have to make sense," said Laila. She shivered, rubbing her hands up and down her arms. She looked at the featureless black sky with the massive metal clouds. "I'm starting to become permanently cold, I think. I wonder where all the stars are. If I could see any stars, maybe I'd know where we are."

"I wouldn't trust the stars any more than I'd trust

anything else here," said Griffin.

"You guys let me know when you're ready to go back," said Ozzie. "I won't even say I told you so. I bet Desda won't either."

"What's the deal with you two? Are you, like, a thing now?" asked Laila.

Ozzie finally sat down, sighing deeply. "She helped me." He paused as if wondering whether that was enough or if he needed to tell them more. He did. "I was terrified. I came down that Black Slide, was dropped into a tiny black cell, and then those freaky things with the pointy eyes were all around me. Experimenting on me. Hurting me." He shook his head. "I was going out of my mind. But Desda was in the cell next to mine. She started talking to me. That's when we learned time was different here. She had gone down the slide maybe hours before me. And yet she'd been here days, maybe weeks, she didn't know. But we talked. We talked a lot. Holy cow, I told her more than I've told anybody ever. It was easier getting through everything knowing that at the end I got to talk to her back in the cells." Ozzie paused at a particularly loud cloudscrape in the sky and scratched at a bit of dried blood on his cheek. "And then one day she escaped."

"And hid in the ceiling," said Griffin.

"Not at first. She tried to help me escape. And Crystal, too, but Crystal was kind of a mess. Desda couldn't figure out how to open the cell. The Merciless use their eyes to open it."

"Ew," said Laila.

"They bend over and scrape them or something on the door. Desda said she'd come back as soon as she figured out how to open it. I don't know how much time passed, but it was easier dealing with what the Merciless were doing to me knowing that she was free and that she was going to come back for me. And she did come back. But she'd changed. One night I heard her voice. And I was so happy. But she was back in the cell next to mine. She said, 'The Black Slide is the only escape.' She didn't say another word to me for days."

"They caught her?" asked Laila.

"No. She had been hiding in the ceiling guts, trying to learn more about the Merciless and find a way out. Eventually she got hungry and hopeless and came down to the Merciless willingly. She stopped talking to me completely after a while."

Ozzie looked at Laila and Griffin for the first time in his story. "That's why she didn't come through the Glare. She didn't care about the pain. She just knew that the red door isn't escape. Only the Black Slide is. She knew that they have to finish their experiments, and then they'll send us back. Catch and release. Like fishing." He sighed and looked down at the ground. "But I didn't listen to her, and

131

now I'm hungry and hurting and cold and waiting for the next monster to eat me."

Griffin saw some sense in what Ozzie was saying. The Painful Place was awful. But he knew about living through awful things. Lived them every day. In his home. At school. Some of it was because of that tall, sad, bleeding boy currently cutting his back up on a black fang rock. The only way Griffin had survived was by running and hiding. And now it seemed running and hiding put him in a worse spot. Maybe it always did.

"I'm sorry" was all Griffin had in him to say.

Ozzie looked chastised by Griffin's response. He fiddled with a dangling strip of his torn sleeve. "I know I was a real jerk back home to you, Griffin. I'm sorry for that." He said the word *sorry* like it was a fact, not like an apology. Griffin liked it better that way. It was also the first time Ozzie had said his name like a name instead of a taunt.

"You were a real jerk." Griffin frowned at Ozzie as hard as he could, but the effort just made Griffin laugh. It rang off the black fangs and must have been the first time anything in that metal-cold landscape had heard such a sound. Laila joined him, almost blowing out a cheek, she laughed so hard, and soon Ozzie let loose as well. Their laughter died quickly, though, and Griffin realized that he was holding his stomach in hunger instead of laughter now, its growl louder than his laugh had been.

"I'm hungry, too," said Laila.

Ozzie nodded. "The food they gave us back in the cells was bad, and I'm still not sure it was food, but I definitely miss it right now."

Griffin could feel himself on the edge of an appalling decision, of admitting that this escape had been a mistake, that the horrors of the Painful Place were better than the horrors of the rest of this world.

But before he could speak up, the landscape spoke. Its voice was another scream of clouds and a few taps on the rocks and ground around them. The rhythm quickly picked up.

"Is it raining?" asked Laila.

"Ouch," said Ozzie.

And then, "Ouch," said Laila.

And then Griffin felt something hit his cast. He looked at the bright yellow fiberglass and, stuck like a fourth exclamation point at the end of Laila's name, was a quivering metal needle. And then another. And then he felt one embed into his shoulder.

"Oh no," said Griffin. "It's raining." And in this place, that meant something excruciating and deadly.

CHAPTER 22

I'm Sorry, but That's the Plan

All three threw their arms over their heads and faces and tried to flatten themselves against the black fangs, choosing to have their backs sliced by the sharp edges of the rock over being perforated by what was falling from the sky. The sharp metal needles sounded like chimes as they sporadically hit the hard metal plain, a grotesquely pretty sound ringing across the dismal and dangerous landscape.

"What do we do?" asked Laila. He heard the wince in her voice and peeked under his yellow arm to see a needle lancing her forearm.

"We're too far away from the Painful Place to get back. We won't make it," said Ozzie as he yanked a needle out of the side of his neck. A tiny trail of blood wended from the wound down to his collarbone. "And I don't know how long we can stay here."

"Not much longer," said Griffin. "We have to get inside the cage forest. It's right over there, and it's the only cover we've got." He stopped there and didn't tell them the other half of his desperate, suddenly formed plan.

"We'll get eaten by those things," said Ozzie. "Or caged. I don't even know. I hate this place."

"It's our only hope," said Griffin. Hope was a strange word to voice out loud in this place, like he'd said a curse word in front of his dad or Ms. Pitts. He could hear the pretty, deadly chimes of the needle rain picking up speed as more needles fell from the black bowl of the sky. If it kept going like this, the black fangs and their arms would be even less shelter than they were now.

"Okay," said Ozzie. "Count of three?"

"No count!" shouted Griffin, springing from the black fangs like a lizard escaping the jaws of a fox and immediately paying for the shout when a needle nicked his lower lip.

They ran. Ran with needles dropping from the sky and embedding into their skin. Ran with arms over their heads to protect their skulls. Ran with hands over their faces to protect their eyes. Griffin could taste the blood in his mouth like he'd knelt and licked the metal ground. Sometimes the needles bounced off with a mere prick of the skin, other times they embedded solidly. The yellow cast he held over his head was spinier than an iguana. He wished the rest of his body were wrapped in an armor-cast to protect him from the needle rain. Even a yellow one covered in Laila's exclamation points.

The red-streaked children crossed the colorless landscape until they arrived at the edge of the cage trees. Every foot of ground inside was within range of one of these cage-boughs. If the plan had been to hide in the forest from both the needle shower and the cage trees, it was a bad plan. There was no safety beneath the clusters of traps at the tops of those poles. When Griffin had first seen the cage forest, he had wondered how they managed to catch anything in their barred jaws, how the creatures of this world were ever foolish enough to stray into this dead zone. But now Griffin felt the needles in his skin and wondered if this was how they caught their prey, driven to the only shelter from these storms across the flat metalscape.

Ozzie and Laila didn't want to be prey. They halted before crossing the border of the forest. "We'll get eaten!" said Ozzie.

And then the needle rain increased. The once pleasant-sounding chime was now a terrifying clatter of metal on metal.

"I'm sorry, but that's the plan," shouted Griffin. And to show them that he was serious, he ran right into that forest like it was any other forest back home, slapping the pole-trunks as he passed. He made it about twenty steps before one of those trees bent its cages at him and snapped him up into its metal jaws, trapping him behind a smile of iron-bar teeth.

CHAPTER 23

What's Wrong with My Skin?

The intense fear at seeing those ribbed jaws coming at him was sharp but brief. The cage-bough snapped shut around Griffin and lifted him into the air, where it became a simple cage in a clump of cages again, a simple cage that doubled as shelter. The relief from the needle storm was immediate and spread warmly throughout Griffin's body.

Griffin could hear the needles pounding the metal top of the cage-bough furiously, trying to porcupine the cage, but they bounced off to the ground like so many lost paper clips, the top of the cage shielding him from death by a thousand pricks from the sky.

Laila and Ozzie quickly understood. They made it about the same distance into the cage-forest and were snapped up by two other cage trees.

"Now what?" asked Ozzie, leaning against the bars

138

and pulling needles from his arms and shoulders and legs. He had to shout to be heard over the deadly deluge.

Laila was doing the same. "I don't even care."

Griffin didn't admit that he hadn't thought beyond being eaten. He'd only planned as far as escaping the needle storm. He rubbed a slick of blood off his face and lay back against the bars. He wanted to close his eyes and sleep, but the tiny stabs in his back told him he needed to extract all the needles from his skin first.

So the three of them sat in their cages, high above the ground, pulling needles from their bodies, hungry and tired and hopeless, their ears hurting from the clatter around them, but not paying too much attention to it because it was one more hurt atop a body full of aches and soreness and pain.

Eventually, the needle storm slackened, the harsh staccato losing its rhythm and then suddenly silencing. Beautiful quiet and relief from pain was all it took to turn his small cage into a paradise. Griffin looked below and saw the ground covered in metal needles, sort of like pine needles carpeting the floors of forests back home, but you didn't have to worry about pine needles piercing your feet as you walked. He wondered if Merciless kids got days off school for needle storms, like they got snow days back home.

"What if these aren't trees?" asked Laila, who had pulled all her needles out and was lying on her back on the small cage floor, her legs bent and her arms lolling through the bars. "Maybe they're traps set by the Merciless for runaways. Maybe we set off an alarm and they're coming to get us right now. That's why they didn't chase us. It's easier to wait until we're packaged up and ready for delivery."

"That would be awesome," said Ozzie. "Like waiting at a bus stop instead of walking all the way back and getting killed by the next deadly thing in this place. I'm tired of it." He kicked the cage-bough in the teeth. The cage-bough didn't react. "I've been lasered and chewed and cut and stabbed and sliced and swallowed. I don't want to experience any more terror verbs."

Laila laughed. "Terror verbs."

Griffin didn't laugh and didn't like Laila laughing at Ozzie's joke. Besides, he was getting distracted by how itchy the skin under his cast was. The doctor had warned him about that. Said the material could irritate his skin, but that he could insert the eraser end of a pencil into the top of the cast and scratch the itch, as long as he did it gently. Good advice for a fifth grader inside a classroom. Bad advice for a fifth grader trapped inside a living cage in an insane world.

"What made you think of this plan?" asked Laila.

"Amazon lava lizards," said Griffin.

"Of course, reptiles," said Laila.

"I don't understand," said Ozzie.

"Amazon lava lizards live in South America. They depend on certain cactuses that grow there to live, and the cactuses depend on them to live, too. It's called symbiosis. The cactus provides food and water and protection for the lizard, and the lizard helps the cactus reproduce by eating its seeds, carrying them around, and then passing them through its digestive system to grow somewhere else."

"Gross," said Ozzie. "I'm not eating—or passing—this thing's seeds." He gave the bar-teeth a shake with both fists.

"I'd eat anything right now," said Laila.

He looked down at the ground, with its fur of needles. "I wonder what happens to all the needles? They can't just stay here; the whole place would be covered in needles. Unless it's a rare event. Which, with our luck, it might've been."

"Maybe they dissolve," said Laila. "Or maybe something eats them."

"I don't want to run into a Needle-Eater," said Ozzie.

Griffin noticed a needle in his leg that he'd missed and pulled it out. His pants were so shredded from Merciless claws and sword grass and sky needles that they weren't

much better than shorts at this point. And he was starting to understand what Laila had meant by "permanently
cold."

But the itch was getting worse than the cold. Worse
than the burn in his belly. And it wasn't just his yellow
arm. His other arm itched, his face itched, his head itched,
his legs itched. Everything itched. He looked at his good
arm and saw the skin reddening.

"What's wrong with my skin?" he heard Laila ask.

"Yeah, mine's on fire," said Ozzie, scratching roughly
at the back of his neck.

Griffin thought of the toothy, venomous Gila monster
that lived in the southwest US and Mexico. "The needles
must have been coated with poison. Or maybe the metal
itself is poisonous." That's all he had. Guesses at the reasons. No guesses at the solution.

They heard a familiar sound, rocks grinding on metal
forming words without breath.

"The cage trees are digesting you."

CHAPTER 24

Watch Out for These Things

Griffin looked down through the bars of his cage, expecting to see Gutter, the only Merciless that had spoken English to him, but the Merciless below was different. It was dressed in the usual shiny black tight-sleeved robe, but instead of the strip dangling from its neck, it had a black sash from shoulder to opposite hip. And its round white head was covered in veins of metal, like frozen lightning. Its eye-cones were aimed at him, and it didn't seem to be afraid of the cage trees.

"I was right. They are Merciless traps," said Laila, scratching at her skin violently.

"No, soft child," the Merciless rumbled, moving its eye cones to her. "What you called cage trees, we call . . ." And it let loose a short string of unintelligible growls and screams. "They grow here naturally. Like rocks."

143

Nothing here looks natural, was Griffin's first thought. *Rocks grow here?* was his second. Before he could voice either, the Merciless continued.

"After they catch their prey, it is disintegrated and absorbed. It takes a long time. Not for soft children, though. You will be fast.

I'm being digested alive was Griffin's third thought, like a bird inside a Burmese python. He had an image of himself dissolving in a dark stomach and panicked enough to rattle the bars. "Get us out!" he shouted. The Merciless didn't react. It looked like it was enjoying the scene. Griffin stopped attacking his cage, embarrassed.

"Why aren't they attacking you?" Laila asked the Merciless.

"They will," said the Merciless. It stepped back, closer to a cage tree. Five seconds later, a cage-bough above it opened and shot toward the Merciless. Before anybody could warn it, the Merciless turned, the sound of buzzy microphone feedback pierced the air, and a red field of energy enveloped the cage-bough. It shook and pulled back slowly, not even shutting back into a cube, just hanging limp with its jaws open, like a cage cut in half. The Merciless showed them the same disc-shaped weapon that the Merciless in the rafters had pointed at them. "But that should teach them. The close ones, anyway."

144

"Help us," said Ozzie. "We'll go back. We won't fight or anything. Just get us out of here."

The Merciless shifted its eye-cones among the three cages, like it was playing eeny, meeny, miney, mo. Griffin almost laughed at the ludicrousness of the idea, but even that glimmer of amusement was squelched as the air around him turned red and his body stiffened in the familiar and paralyzing pain of the Glare. After a slightly shorter eternity of pain than he'd experienced in the red door, he was thudding painfully to the metal ground, the needles cushioning his fall. The ones that didn't puncture him, at least. Dangling above him were the slack jaws of the cage he'd just been inside of.

A pair of screams from Laila and Ozzie, and they were on the ground, too, writhing and shouting. The Merciless waited until they had stopped.

"Follow me," it said.

Unlike Ozzie, Griffin wasn't sure he wanted to return to the Painful Place, but right now the Merciless was headed out of this striped forest, and that was at least a direction he could get on board with.

It was hard walking on the needles. Only slightly better than if the sky had rained ball bearings. And a fall meant more needles jabbing through their skin. The Merciless didn't seem to have a problem with the needles, though.

The needles bent and warped under its boots. The being must have been really heavy. Griffin remembered what Laila had said about running into one.

They quickly made it out of the forest, only to be surprised by the Merciless walking in the opposite direction from the Painful Place.

Ozzie spoke up. "Shouldn't we be going the other way?"

The Merciless didn't respond. Just kept walking in front of them. Shouldn't it be behind them, forcing them in a direction with the Glare weapon in its hand? It was almost like it didn't care whether they followed or not. Either way, the open air felt good on Griffin's skin, and he could already feel the itches subsiding. Eventually they were back on bare terrain again and didn't have to worry about falling on needles.

They passed a cluster of mound monsters glimmering in the cloud light, so Griffin took the opportunity to try to talk to the Merciless and find out where they were going. He matched the being's pace and said casually, like he was telling it about one of his reptiles back home, "We almost got eaten by those things." He lifted his cast to show its mangled condition.

The Merciless turned its head to the hard white mound. "Doubtful."

"Yeah, they didn't seem to like our taste."

"Too soft, like decayed meat," said the Merciless. It didn't elaborate. At least it was sort of an explanation. Griffin dropped back next to Laila.

She drew her head closer to Griffin. "I don't know if we should trust it."

"What else can we do?" asked Griffin.

"Watch out for these things," grumble-shrieked the Merciless. It pointed its Glare at a smooth flat circle in the metal ground that was almost impossible to distinguish from the plain. The Merciless shot staticky red pain into the center, and the smooth flatness churned into a dry, boiling quicksand, like a pool of iron fillings moving to a magnet. A large, hinged pair of pincers surfaced and opened in an electronic scream before disappearing under again, the pool solidifying back into hard flatness.

"I say we trust it for now," said Griffin as they gave the flat circle a wide berth.

He had second thoughts about that idea an hour later when the Merciless led them to a thick outcropping of black fang rocks. Nestled within them was a small building about the size of a cabin, that looked like it was made of the same rock. It had a small opening on its broadest side. The Merciless dragged two metal-tipped fingers across its shiny black sash, and a glowing red field instantly covered the opening. Another red door that didn't lead to Griffin's house, another red door of pain. The Merciless waved them through it.

CHAPTER 25

Soft Dies

"You ruined a perfectly good doorway," said Ozzie. Despite the cold and the joke, Griffin could see a shine of sweat on the boy's forehead. Griffin wiped his own forehead. He was feeling it, too. He couldn't do the Glare. Not like that. Getting shot with it briefly and by surprise in the cage tree forest had been much easier than walking willingly into it and staying in it.

"The Glare is how you enter," said the Merciless.

"We'd rather not," said Laila. "It's such a beautiful night. We should stay out here." Griffin caught her looking at the solid black sky uncertainly, as if weighing whether she would be able to run through the portal if needles shot from it again.

The Merciless grumble-screamed something in its own language and scratched its sash. The Glare disappeared. The

Merciless waved them inside again, and the three entered quickly, afraid it was going to turn the Glare on while they were walking through the doorway.

Which it sort of did.

No sooner had they gotten inside than the interior of the small building bloomed red.

Griffin yelped and threw his arms over his head, falling against something solid and hitting the floor. But nothing happened. Nothing painful happened, at least, other than the bruise he'd just earned. He heard rocks screaming and metal twisting and looked up to see the Merciless itself trapped in the Glare. Laila and Ozzie looked like mirror images of Griffin, leaning back against the furniture they had stumbled on, gazing at the torture of the Merciless in horror, both bathed in the red light of the Glare. Although the Glare wasn't the bright red that Griffin knew from the Painful Place. It was paler. Almost pink.

Finally, the Merciless made it through, lurching inside and placing its hands on its knees and pointing its eyes-cones briefly at them. "Soft children," it said.

It walked over to a wall and ran its eyes across it, the scratching sound making Griffin wince. A light came on in the cabin that canceled out the pale red glow of the Glare. The cabin was small and looked a lot like the area outside the building. The floor was metal, and scattered around it were hunks of sharp black rock like frozen beanbags. Flat surfaces on the rocks suggested that they could be used as furniture. A counter ran against one wall with various devices on it, below which were a set of metal cabinets.

"Sit," said the Merciless, and the three obeyed, although it took them a while to find the least uncomfortable position on the uncomfortable furniture. Griffin sat on a hard-angled boulder, crossing his legs atop it so that they wouldn't brush against the sharp edges. Laila and Ozzie chose their own rocks.

The Merciless opened one of the metal cabinets and pulled out a handful of baseball-sized stones, each of a slightly different hue. The colors were as pale as old post-cards, but what the being held in its hands was still more color than Griffin had seen in the entire Painful Place. Outside of the Glare, of course. It dropped the stones into a black cylinder on the counter, which vibrated the room with a harsh roar that was only second to a Merciless caught in the Glare as the worst sound Griffin had ever heard. When it ended, the Merciless poured a thick chunky gray liquid from the cylinder into three metal bowls and passed them out. "Eat before it solidifies," it said.

Griffin looked in his bowl and found a shimmery paste that looked like bad oatmeal. It didn't look edible, but the warm bowl in his hand was enough to set his stomach groaning. "What is it?"

"Minerals," said the Merciless.

"Minerals?" asked Laila. "You want us to eat rocks?"

"Calcium. Sodium. Potassium. Iron. Also vitamins. What your soft bodies need to stay alive."

"And it's going to solidify? Like back into rock?" asked Griffin.

"Yes," said the Merciless.

"What if it solidifies inside us?" Griffin imagined his body full of quick-dry cement and almost threw the bowl across the cabin.

"Your body heat should keep it unsolid until it absorbs the nutrients."

"Yuck. I don't think I can eat rock paste," said Laila.

A gross sound caused Griffin and Laila to look over at Ozzie, who was scraping the last bits of mineral paste out of his bowl with his fingers and then sucking on them. "What?" he said. "It's what they gave us in the cells. You get used to it. Plus, all our food back home has vitamins and minerals in it."

"I never thought of it as rocks," said Laila, staring uncertainly at the inside of her bowl.

Seeing Ozzie dig in with his fingers gave Griffin the confidence to try. That and his stomach yelling at him. He scooped a lump of it onto his index finger and stuck it in his mouth. It was grainy and warm and tasted like metal, but it was the first thing he'd had in his mouth in he didn't know how long, so he wolfed it down like ice cream.

While they ate, the Merciless stared at them in silence. Griffin almost preferred running from the Merciless over hanging out with one. Asking a question meant hearing its windless torment of a voice answering the question. Looking into its face meant imagining those silver cones poking into his eyes. And the way it held its white boulder of a head, it seemed like it wanted to headbutt him. Maybe if he knew its name, it would be easier. "What's your name?"

"Leech."

That didn't help at all.

"Did you follow us from the Painful Place?"

"What are you talking about?"

"Big black building. Giant slide sticking out of its roof?" said Laila.

"That is the Forge."

"Then what's the Painful Place?" asked Griffin.

"Everything is the Painful Place," said Leech, and Griffin thought he could hear a rumble of pride in that rockslide of a sentence.

"That makes so much sense," said Ozzie.

It did make sense, thought Griffin. The metal ground, the mound monsters, the needle rain, the cage trees. The whole world was the Painful Place. "Did you follow us from the Forge?" asked Griffin.

"No, I am not a Forge Merciless." Leech seemed offended by the question.

153

"What's the Forge for?" asked Laila.

Leech gnashed its metal teeth and stroked the jagged metal veins on its head. "You know nothing." It sat on one of the boulder chairs, rubbing its left leg back and forth across an edge. The sound was a knife being sharpened. "How long do you soft children live?"

It sounded like one of the trick questions Mrs. Pitts often asked in class, and like in class, it took a few moments for one of them to build up the courage to answer it. "My grandma's eighty-seven," said Laila.

"I heard that the oldest person who ever lived hit one hundred twenty-two years," said Ozzie. "That's, like"—he counted rapidly on his fingers a few times—"ten or eleven of me."

"An obscenely short time," said Leech. Griffin thought the Merciless had misunderstood, and almost corrected him, but the next sentence shut him up. "The Merciless live for about fourteen of your centuries. Our oldest get close to two thousand years old. But it was not always that way. We used to be short-lived and decay-prone like you, all soft fetus skin and brittle chalk-stick bone. We learned to harden ourselves to live longer." It rapped its knuckles on his head, making a dull thud.

"I don't get it," said Ozzie. Griffin shrugged at Ozzie to let him know that he wasn't alone.

"Soft dies; hard survives," said Leech. "Rock, metal—these things live forever. Soft things rot fast and go away. Everything on the surface of your planet dies . . . animals, humans, plants. Soft is vulnerable; soft is weak." He aimed his eye-cones at Griffin's bright injury. "The Merciless do not break as easily as you do."

"There's a pile of white powder on the floor of the Forge that would disagree," said Ozzie.

Leech almost shot its eye cones at Ozzie. "We live a long time, but not forever." It stopped scraping its leg on the rock chair and leaned forward. "But we want to live forever. That is why you are here. Many of the Merciless think we may be able to further our quest for immortality by studying you."

"You mean by experimenting on us," said Griffin.

"Yes. That is what the Forge is for."

"Why our world?"

"Your world shares in common many things with the Painful Place," said Leech.

"No way," said Laila. "Your world is metal and rock. We have grass and dirt, leafy trees. Our clouds are fluffy. We have puppies."

"Lakes and oceans and sand," said Ozzie.

"Pillows and couches and sweaters," said Griffin.

"Stress balls and slime," added Ozzie.

155

"You know nothing," said Leech. "Your world pretends to be soft. Soft grass. Soft dirt. Soft water. That is all skin. It is rock and metal below. You are that way as well. Your shell is soft and fragile, but you have hardness inside. Your heart can be made stone. Your spirit can be steeled. And your world does that to you. Hardens you. You are young. Maybe you do not know. Or maybe you do. School. Parents. Siblings. Bullies. Authority figures. Enemies." Griffin tried not to stare too intently at anything. "It is why we choose children your age. You are at the edge of starting to harden. The older you get, the more difficult your life gets and the harder you will get. We can speed that process with our experiments. But you only harden to make it through your short life. You do not do it to extend your life."

Griffin was uncomfortable with what Leech was saying. He didn't understand all of it, but it sounded a lot like something his dad always said that Griffin hated hearing: "Life is hard."

"How did you get us all down the Black Slide without anybody knowing?" asked Laila. "Did you hypnotize the adults like you did us?"

"We anesthetized the area. Made things numb and fuzzy for your adults, made it difficult for them to perceive and think. It will wear off when we return you."

"You do send us back!" Ozzie smiled at Laila and

Griffin like he had just eliminated them both in a game of dodgeball.

"Why would we want to keep you here?" It shifted its eye-cones to Griffin's bright injury and motioned at Griffin's cast like it wanted to touch it. "That was not done here."

"I got it falling out of your Black Slide."

"You opened the Black Slide?"

"What?"

"You were the first to enter it?"

Griffin nodded.

"For the Black Slide to connect the Painful Place to your world, it needs to be opened from your side. A soft child has to enter it first." Griffin glanced at Laila as Leech ran a sharp finger along one of its head veins. "Opening the Black Slide is a level of pain I can only aspire to. Tell me about it."

"No," said Griffin. He rubbed his own head. Leech's voice was giving him a headache and a toothache at the same time.

Leech nodded its head slowly. "Private pain is more powerful."

"I still don't get where you come in," said Laila. "Why are you helping us?"

"Because I need you to help me destroy the Black Slide."

CHAPTER 26

It Has Blunted Our Eyes

Griffin felt like the most selfish clod in the world—any world, his own or the Painful Place. Probably both. The entire time that he had been trapped in cells and swinging from ceilings and pushing through the Glare and running across the metal plains away from monsters, he had thought only of escaping this place. Of getting him and Laila and even Ozzie out of this mace head of a world. Other than that brief, futile moment when he found Crystal in a cell, everything he had done was just to get back home to his mom and his reptiles and his blue sky and green grass. He had never once thought about stopping what was happening. Preventing it from happening again. Maybe his insides were already full of cement.

"You want to destroy the Black Slide?" asked Laila.

"The Merciless hang all of our hopes of achieving

158

immortality on these experiments. It has blunted our eyes to other ideas, other paths, other possibilities that I believe will be more successful. I think the Black Slides have made us softer, not harder. And if we shut them all down, we could find the real path to immortality."

"Black Slides*ssss*? Shut *them* all down?" Griffin imagined Black Slides in playgrounds all over the country, all over the world, sucking down children into this terrible place. "There's more than one?"

"Yes."

"All over our world?" asked Griffin.

"No. There is only one Forge for Earth."

"Lucky us," said Ozzie.

"But yours is not the only world that we experiment on. We have many Forges, and before yours was the Earth Forge, it was a Forge for another place. The Merciless believe that anywhere we find life, we might find the answer to eternal life. That is the dogma here."

"And you don't believe that," said Laila, like she didn't believe him the first time he said it.

"My ideas are considered . . ." It chewed wetly on its black tongue for a moment. "Sacrilege."

"I like your ideas," said Ozzie.

"I was stripped of my position at what is now the Earth Forge because of this belief. But I *know* the Black Slides are the soft way. So after I was banished from the Forge, I stayed and kept watch over it. Waiting for an opportunity to destroy it." Its eye-cones swung in an arc that encompassed all three of them. "You are that opportunity."

"You've been watching us?" asked Laila.

"Since your escape."

"If we help you destroy the Black Slide . . . our Black Slide, can you . . . can you get us back home? Get everybody back to Osshua?" All that sudden guilt and disappointment and shock and shame that Griffin felt coalesced into that single hope.

"I can send every soft child from your school back. And then I will destroy the Black Slide and nobody in your world will ever have to come to the Painful Place again. And then I will find a way to destroy the other Black Slides to the other worlds."

"What do we have to do?" asked Griffin, his resolve as hard as the chair he was sitting on. As hard as the rock walls of the building he was sitting in. As hard as the metal ground of the world he was stuck in.

"I need you to get me inside the Forge," said Leech.

"You don't know where the front Glare is?" asked Ozzie.

Leech grabbed its black sash in one metal-tipped hand and lifted it, while grabbing a metal fitting on its robe with the other. The robe opened, baring its chest, a chest that was as ice-white as its round head, with bits of metal embedded in it. In the center of its chest was a dark hole about the size of a coin.

"Why are you flashing us?" asked Griffin.

"As part of my banishment, they opened me. I cannot pass through the Glare and survive."

"You took it okay here," said Laila, nodding at the pale red luminescence filling the doorway. "I mean, you took it screaming and writhing, but that seems to count as okay here."

"That Glare is at a lower power than what is used at the Forge. Even lower than a handheld Glare." It closed its robe and fished out the metal disc weapon from a hidden pocket. Griffin flinched despite himself. "I have been trying to build tolerance to the Glare or to find a way to block the hole in my chest from it. So far, I have failed. The Glare can get inside me and kill me. That is the opposite of immortality."

"So how do we get you in?" asked Griffin, who was feeling a little queasy on the subject of body holes.

"I will you tell you the plan. But first, I must gather the others." It stood up like the conversation was over.

"Wait. What others?" asked Griffin.

"I am not the only Merciless who believes the Black

161

Slides need to be destroyed, not the only outcast who has been opened and is as fragile as a cracked egg."

"You're going to leave us here?" asked Ozzie.

"Yes. But when I return, we will head to the Forge and close the Black Slide."

"Forever," said Griffin.

"Forever," said Leech, the syllables of the word clashing together in an explosion of rock and metal.

CHAPTER 27

In Exchange for Dissolving Us Whole

After Leech screamed its way through the pale, low-powered Glare and back out into the metal plains of the Painful Place, the three looked at each other from their stony seats inside the stony cabin. Griffin's belly felt comfortably heavy for the first time since sliding into this place.

"We're not going to trust it, right?" asked Laila.

Her question surprised Griffin. "Why wouldn't we?"

"Because we can't even trust the rocks and the trees in this place. How are we going to trust any of the Merciless?"

"It treated us better than any of the Merciless have treated me so far," said Ozzie.

"What other choice do we have?" asked Griffin. "Wander the metal plains until we're skeletons? Get rained on until we bleed to death? Or dissolved by trees or swallowed

163

by metal pools with giant pincers?"

"We *could* go back without Leech," said Ozzie. "Do what Desda said we should have done in the first place."

"Let them experiment on us?" asked Griffin.

"Sure, maybe. Even Leech says the Merciless just want to learn if we have what they need," said Ozzie.

"You know what they did to you. You want to go through that again?" asked Griffin.

"If it's the only way to get back home, I can put up with anything," said Ozzie.

"So we have three options," said Laila, holding up three fingers. "Option One." Two of the fingers folded. "We keep wandering the Painful Place. The upside to that is that we're not trapped, not being tortured, and who knows what we'll find. The downside to that is death and dismemberment in a hostile landscape. Option Two." Two fingers in the air now. "We ditch Leech, go back to the Forge by ourselves, let them conduct their experiments, and go home. Treat it like school, basically. Just . . . much worse. Upside there is it might be a path home. The downside is, well, the experiments."

Laila raised three fingers back in the air. "Option Three, we help Leech take down the Black Slide. Upsides are we go home, we rescue everybody, and the Black Slide never bothers anybody again. The downside is who knows

164

if we can trust Leech, what his plan is, or if that plan will even work."

She stopped, waiting for Griffin or Ozzie to say something, but neither did. The three sat in silence in the black cottage, which was spare and uncluttered except for their bowls balanced on the rock furniture. Griffin had eaten most of his rock paste, but what was left had solidified into flat, gray stone like frozen milk in a cereal bowl. He suddenly realized that Leech hadn't told them how long he'd be gone. Hours? Days? Weeks? They still hadn't figured out how to tell time here, so maybe it didn't matter. Those were the thoughts going through his head after Laila laid out the options—not because he was avoiding choosing, but because he already knew which plan they had to do. He just didn't know how to convince Laila and Ozzie if they disagreed. Finally, after tapping the rock in his bowl to get their attention, he said, "We have to trust Leech."

"Why?" asked Laila.

"We have to try to save everybody," said Griffin. "Remember Crystal in that cell? She looked so . . . different. So empty. We have to help all the fifth graders."

"I'd love to save everybody," said Laila. "But I just don't know if Leech is trustworthy."

"Even the cage trees helped us when we needed it," said Griffin.

"In exchange for dissolving us whole."

"Point for Laila," said Ozzie. She rolled her eyes at him. "If you want my vote," he continued, "I kind of don't care, as long as we go back to the Forge. I figure if Leech's plan works, great. If it doesn't, we'll just get sent back the hard way. Basically, I'm voting for not wandering the death-scape out here anymore."

"Let's destroy the Black Slide," said Griffin to Laila.

Laila looked at him for a long moment, then nodded. "Okay."

Ozzie let out a dreadful moan of a yawn wide enough to loosen his jawbone. Griffin started his own before Ozzie even finished. They were all tired. Full and seemingly safe and definitely exhausted.

They tried to find decent places to lie down. A few of the boulders were longer, like they maybe passed for couches or beds in this terrible world. But they couldn't sleep on them, tired as they were.

They ended up clumping cozily together in a corner on the floor, using each other for pillows and warmth. Sleep was instantaneous, and they slept for a very long time and would probably have doubled that time had they not been awoken by the screaming of the tortured.

CHAPTER 28

We're Going to Fail Badly

Leech and two other Merciless stood in the stone cabin, fresh from the weakened torments of the reduced Glare. One of the new Merciless had curved spikes on each side of its head like shiny devil horns, and the other looked like a thick pole had been shoved through its temples. Like Leech, both wore shiny black sashes across their chests. Leech was muttering rocks and metal in its own language at the two Merciless, who spun their pale boulder heads to aim their eye-cones at all three of them in turn, but mostly at Griffin. He could guess what Leech was saying: *Here are the soft children. That one opened the Black Slide.*

Laila was sitting beside him on the floor, wiping drool off her chin and trying to blink herself into clarity. Ozzie was standing by the counter with a few pale-colored rocks in his hands. He was apparently hungry enough to get up and try to figure out how to dissolve the stones. Although now he looked like he was ready to use them as weapons against the Merciless filling the room if he had to. Griffin had been winged by stones thrown by Ozzie before. They stung. One time it had even made his leg bleed. Griffin had almost forgotten that the kid was a jerk. Back home, at least.

Leech's rumbles and screeches ripped through English words now. "Are you prepared to march to the Forge?"

"There's only three of you?" asked Laila, still doubtful of Leech and its unknown plan.

"There are more outside," said Leech.

"How many?" asked Griffin. He didn't know how many of the Merciless were in the Forge, but judging by size of the building, there could have been hundreds working there.

"Three thousand," said Leech.

"Three thousand!" said Laila. She was up now, her chin dry, her eyes open wide and leaning against the smooth part of a rock couch.

"We have an army!" yelled Ozzie, almost juggling the rocks in his hands. "We can flatten that place. I've always wanted to be part of an army."

Leech rattled off gravel and BBs to Horn Head and Pole Head, their eye-cones almost touching, apparently confused by the exuberance of the soft children. "Halt," said Leech. "My grasp of math in your language is fleshy. Not three thousand. Thirty rebel Merciless is what we have."

A staccato of loud thuds echoed in the cabin as the rocks fell from Ozzie's limp hands. A near curse word and a smack came from Laila as she punched her palm. An "Ouch" spat from Griffin as he flopped carelessly onto a rock seat, scraping his thigh on an edge and further shredding his pants. It was getting to the point that he'd need to check to make sure he had nice underwear on. He gave a quick peek. Yellow with green cartoon lizards on it. Great.

"Your reactions are strange," said Leech.

"We're going to fail badly," said Laila.

"How are thirty of you going to take out that massive Forge and all the Merciless inside?" asked Griffin.

"Four hundred work in the Forge at a time. Wait." Leech cast its eye-cones at the ceiling and clenched its jaws a couple of times, and Griffin grew hopeful that it was bad math again. "Yes, that is correct. Four hundred." Griffin shook his head. Hope flattened easily on the metal ground of the Painful Place. Leech continued. "But that is how many it takes to run the Forge. It takes very few to make the Forge not run."

"How do you know?" asked Laila.

"All my Merciless have worked in a Forge before. We know how to destroy it. You just have to get us in, and then stay out of our way until we have control of it."

"How can you be sure?" she pressed.

"We have done it before."

"How?"

"At one Forge, the Glare malfunctioned. It gave us the opening we needed."

"And you sent everybody back?" asked Laila.

"We did. And we will do it for you. And then we will destroy the Black Slide."

"Oh no," said Griffin, staring at the faint glow from the doorway.

"What?" asked Ozzie.

"We have to get them in. I just realized what that means." Griffin looked at Leech, but could read nothing in its stone face and eye cones. "We have to go back through the Glare, don't we?"

"Once inside, you can shut it down for us," said Leech.

"Back through the Glare," said Griffin again.

CHAPTER 29

Getting Hurt's My New Thing

The tiny army of soft children and punctured Merciless hid in a large outcropping of black fangs. In the distance, past humps of mound monsters and smaller clusters of black fangs and sharp grass was the big black bulk of the Forge. The Black Slide angled dizzyingly above it like the thick string of a moon-sized balloon, lost in the darkness above the glowing metal clouds spraying sparks as they scraped and screamed and flashed past each other.

Griffin still felt uncomfortable being surrounded by so many Merciless. Especially since only Leech spoke English. The others leered and screeched and growled at them. Griffin got it the worst, as they would regularly point at his cast and clack their pointy metal teeth at him or extend their tiny black tongues in his direction. Besides Pole Head and Horn Head, there was Shark Fin Head and Buzzsaw

171

Head and Checkerboard Head. Lots of others with metal embedded in their craniums. They all wore the shiny, tight-sleeved robes that seemed to be the uniform in the Painful Place. The only difference now was that the rebels had exchanged the shiny black sashes across their chests for shiny black strips dangling from their necks.

So many Merciless, but so few compared to what they were up against in that big black building that from this distance blended with the dark sky.

Their trek across the metal plain with the Merciless had been uneventful compared to their escape across it. They knew a little more about what to avoid now, and the Merciless showed them all new terrors to stay away from. Griffin wondered if the Merciless could ever just go for an afternoon walk in this world. Or if there ever was an afternoon. The black sky had not lightened even a little since their escape from the Forge.

But crossing the deadly metal plain was only the commute. Griffin was still unsure what the rebel Merciless planned to do. Leech had told him it was too complicated to explain to a soft child. But at this point, sitting among the black fangs and staring at the Forge, it was less the uncertainty of the plan he was uncomfortable with. It was the certain part. And that was less discomfort and more outright terror.

They had to go through the Glare again.

At least, Laila, Ozzie, and Griffin had to. Although Leech hadn't told them how exactly they were going to shut the Glare down yet, either.

As they watched the Forge from their nest of fangs, a white light shone on the horizon. A train from the city.

That was good news. It meant Leech was right about the schedule at the Forge. He had predicted a train at about this time. For the plan to work, they would have to sneak in during a dead spot of activity, when no Merciless were exiting or entering, and no train would be exchanging passengers. Time was different for the Merciless, but Leech had attempted to make the conversion for them. Half an hour. That was how much time they had to cross the plain, suffer the Glare, and turn it off.

It was almost time. Both for the impossible part of the plan that they all knew about, and the worst part of the plan that only Griffin did. Because on the march here, he had realized something. And now he was going to say something. "All of us don't have to go through the Glare," he said to Laila and Ozzie, while keeping his eyes on the Forge.

"What do you mean?" asked Ozzie hopefully, peering around a black fang as if what Griffin had said had changed the landscape to a grassy field at the end of a rainbow.

"Only one of us needs to shut it down. The other two can come in with the rebels."

"I hadn't thought of that," said Laila.

"Me either," said Ozzie. He shrugged. "Rock, paper, scissors?"

Griffin shook his head. "No. I'm going."

"Why you?" asked Laila.

"Because . . ." Griffin had to search for an answer because he didn't want to tell them the real reason. "Because I want to." He didn't want to. But he didn't want it to be Laila or Ozzie, either.

"I don't like it," said Laila. "Feels a lot like you at the top of the Black Slide on the playground and me and Ozzie watching from below."

"Time to move," said Leech from behind Griffin, making him almost leap to the top of a black fang in surprise. "You will need this." He held out a fist, and Griffin placed his open hand beneath it. Leech dropped two silvery items into his palm, and Griffin held them up to his face, not quite understanding what they were.

And then he did understand what they were, and dropped them in disgust.

The two severed eye cones clinked as they hit the metal ground and then rolled rapidly in opposite directions.

"Yuck. Why did you put those in my hand?"

174

"You need those to turn off the Glare," said Leech. When nobody moved to pick up the eye-cones, it explained, "Just inside the Glare is a control console. It looks like a small table. That is where you turn it off."

"I saw that thing," said Griffin. "There are no controls on it. It's just flat and blank."

"Our eyes see along a wider spectrum than your wet, sunken jellies," said Leech. "The controls are there; you just cannot see them."

Griffin flashed back to the dais on the painground and the tables wrapped in Black Slide leather. He had been right after all. It was a control center.

"You guys see different than us?" said Ozzie. "Does the Painful Place look barren and dark and scary to you too?"

"What am I, a poet?" Leech grumble-screaked. Every word the Merciless said sounded like a bad one, but *poet* sounded like a really bad one.

"If we can't see the controls, how are we supposed to use them?" asked Laila.

"We use our eyes and fingertips on the panels." It held up its metal-tipped hand. "The controls for the door Glare are simple. You need to scratch those eye cones down the center of the black panel. Hold them this far apart." It motioned at the space between its own eye cones. "If it does not work the first time, keep trying. You will get it."

Griffin heard Leech's explanation but was more concerned with Laila's question. He couldn't let her or Ozzie use his revulsion at the eye cones as an excuse for them to go instead. He bent and picked them up off the ground. They felt cold and a little oily. On the flat sides were a series of broken prongs covered in white dust. He almost dropped them again. If these beings had managed to build tunnels between worlds, couldn't they have mastered the simplicity of buttons and touch screens?

"Use the rock cover as long as you can," said Leech. "Stay away from everything else."

"I know," said Griffin.

"I'll go with you—" said Laila before Griffin cut her off.

"No. No, no, no. I've got this. My broken arm, the Glare, the mound monsters, the cage trees. I'm starting to dig pain. Getting hurt's my new thing." Griffin held up the eye cones and managed not to cringe before shoving them into the pocket of his shredded pants.

Griffin stepped quickly out of the rock outcropping before Laila could protest again and started running across the seamed ground, his club arm pounding him in the ribs. He stopped at the first cluster of black fangs he encountered. The Forge hadn't gotten any bigger, which both dismayed and relieved him. They had set up so far away

176

because they needed a large enough outcropping to hide Leech's "army." Maybe it was too far away. Maybe it was impossible to get everything done in half an hour starting from that distance. Maybe he was just slow. He imagined Ozzie passing him while he hid behind a rock and saying without breaking stride or a sweat, "We were going to let you be the hero, but you're way too slow."

But Ozzie didn't pass him, and Griffin kept running from rock to rock, steering clear of mound monsters, and soon enough the black building with the angled tube on its roof grew larger, and too soon that glowing red door was visible. He stopped behind one of the outbuildings, lungs burning, legs burning, everything burning like he had run through the Glare already. Now was the real test, though. Would he be able to do it? Just walk back into the Glare? His bravery had been all words so far. The last time he had entered that Glare, he had followed Laila's lead. The last time, he'd believed escape was on the other side.

He knew that he at least had enough courage to walk up to the door, but before he could try, a dark movement at the edge of his vision stopped him as still as a fang rock. He was caught. He had been too slow, and now a Merciless was about to capture him. He risked turning his head to look for the source of the movement.

Nothing. The landscape was a frozen video game

screen. Two rounded black rocks like moles on the face of the metal were the only things in the area where he had seen the movement, and they were far too small for anyone to hide behind, even a Merciless.

As he stared at the two rocks, each about the size of a Galápagos tortoise, trying to figure out what had tricked him, one of the rocks shot into the air with an ear-ripping whistle. It ascended so high he could see its underside, where a cluster of long metallic tentacles dangled. A cluster of long metallic tentacles aimed right at him.

CHAPTER 30

Smashed into People Puddles

Griffin's neck bent back painfully for a face full of black sky before whiplashing down for a face burn on the shiny metal ground. He hadn't heard anybody behind him. Had barely felt hands push against his shoulder blades. He burned his good palm in the fall as well, and banged one of his kneecaps bad enough he grabbed it and rolled onto his back with a grunt.

The tentacled rock missed him, hitting the spot where he had been standing with a force that broke a pair of nearby fang rocks and seemed to shake the entire Painful Place. The impact created a craterous dent in the ground, with the black, tentacled rock at its center. Had Griffin not been pushed, he would have been pudding.

"Told you. Can't trust anything in this place," said Laila, standing above him.

She took his good hand and helped him up, just in time for another loud whistle to lance the air. They caught a glimpse of the underside of the other tentacled rock high above them, its metal roots squirming hungrily beneath it. Laila ran, tugging Griffin by his hand, and the thing landed exactly where they had been standing, the ground heaving with the massive shake of an earthquake and collapsing into a deep dent. Griffin saw two white circles like eyes flutter open on the rock at the center of the crater and then quickly close.

"What are these things?" he asked. "They look like octopuses."

"You want a nature lesson right now?" asked Laila. "We need to get through the Glare without getting smashed into people puddles."

She pulled him toward the red glow, but Griffin yanked his hand out of hers. "No. You're not going through the Glare. Just me."

"I'm not letting you go through that by yourself," said Laila.

"You have to."

"I don't."

Another whistle cut through their quarrel, and a tentacled rock dropped in front of them, knocking them both on their butts and cratering the metal where they had been about to step. Their argument had saved them. Griffin scrabbled at the ground and braced himself for the tentacles of the creature to shoot out of the crater and grab them, but none came. Apparently, the thing liked to smash its prey into paste first.

"Maybe it's safer in the Glare than out here," said Griffin, looking uncertainly at Laila. She twisted her lips but didn't say anything. He could pretend any reason he wanted to for her going through the Glare. She was going through for her own reason.

Another whistle and both Laila and Griffin were on their feet again. This time, it was Griffin leading Laila by the hand. They circled around the crater and pulled up so close to the Glare that their skin looked red and what was left of his yellow cast looked orange. But he couldn't allow himself the luxury of pausing too long to gather himself before entering. He let go of Laila's hand and walked into the Glare.

Pain. All pain. Every pain. Everywhere pain. Pain like having every tooth drilled at the same time by a chain saw. Pain like his organs were being ripped from his body by sharp hooks. Pain like his heart was going to explode. Like his eyeballs were going to explode. Like his lungs and his brain were going to explode. Pain like all his limbs were being chewed and pulled apart by Komodo dragons, each

181

strand of his muscle popping like a broken guitar string. Pain like the fire of cobra poison melting his veins and seizing his heart. Pain like he had never experienced the Glare before.

And then he was inside the building, and cool, sweet relief flooded every particle of his body and mind so that his mouth, gaping and screaming in the Glare, was now stretched into a wide smile and the exit hatch of a loud belly laugh.

The laugh was short-lived, though, choked by the metal-studded loops lowered around his neck by the large group of Merciless waiting for him.

CHAPTER 31

I'll Get Rid of My Reptiles

Ozzie had never gone into detail to Griffin about the experiments he'd suffered on the painground, but even if he had, there was no way he could have explained the true agony that was the Forge.

Every day, or every whatever-passed-for-days here, Griffin was walked from his cell via one of those choker poles through the dense white fog that swirled and shifted around the painground like living snowdrifts. Leech had told him that the fog was a by-product of the Black Slide, of the connection between the two worlds. That was why the fog was only present in the Forge. But that didn't make the roiling whiteness any less spooky. Once on the painground, Griffin was strapped to the grotesque playground equipment, prodded and poked, forced to watch horrific scenes on screens. Every night he was locked in the claustrophobic cell alone and aching and exhausted. He found it hard to believe that he had shared one of these cells with Laila. It barely fit him. He felt like a turtle taped shut and unable to open.

The strangest part was that, lonely and cramped in his cell each night, he could barely remember the experiments. It was like his brain was as foggy as the painground. He knew the devices. Knew that sometimes the Glare was used. Knew that something happened out there every day. But other than vague feelings and images, it was difficult to remember. He kept thinking of the phrase Leech had used—*anesthetized the area*—and thought maybe that's what was happening. Like the Merciless were blocking him from remembering. But even if he couldn't remember, he still dreaded the painground every night.

Worse than the experiments and the cell was being separated from Laila.

He didn't know what had happened to her. After they were captured, he had been taken directly to a cell. The Merciless hadn't even tried to question why he and Laila had returned. Didn't seem to suspect that they were the advance guard of a tiny rebel army. Maybe it seemed obvious to them why Laila and Griffin had come back. Soft children couldn't survive the Painful Place, so of course they'd return. It wasn't too far from the truth.

Griffin tried to call out to the adjacent cells to see if Laila was nearby, but all he heard were the shouts of his classmates in the other cells, telling him to shut up, that screaming and yelling were for the painground. On the painground, he strained to see her in any of the equipment, but soon was distracted by his own torture sessions, the experiments that accelerated the hardening process to give the Merciless more data in their quest for immortality. At the end of each day, he was fed a bowl of the hot rock paste in his cell. He could feel himself growing dull to his situation. Empty. Hardened. The painground and the cell were his only clock hands, his day and night. No school bell, no phone chimes; daytime was the white fog and flashing Glare of the painground, and nighttime was the darkness of his cell.

At first, he held out hope that Ozzie and Leech and the rest of the rebel Merciless would rescue him. But they didn't come. Not his first "night" in the cell. Not his second. Not his third or his fourth or his fifth. The plan had failed.

On what he guessed was the tenth night, Griffin lost it. Full panic. Tired and beat-up and alone and trapped and his nostrils burning from the white fog and anticipating so much more experimentation, he smashed the wall with his cast, his fist, his feet. Tried to yank the metal bars out of the window. Tried to flip the cell on its side by throwing himself against its walls. And then he shouted, not caring what his trapped classmates shouted back. "Mom!" he yelled as loudly as he could. "I'm here! In this box. Can you hear me?" When she didn't respond, he got desperate enough to call for his dad. "Dad! Dad, can you come get me? You weren't so bad. Not really. Not like the Merciless. If you come get me, I'll do anything you want. Keep the house clean. Stay out of your way. I'll get rid of my reptiles!" His cruel father versus the cruel Merciless was something he would have liked to see.

After screaming for a good ten minutes for his mom and his dad and then just in general screaming, he heard his name echo among the cells.

"Griffin!" Was that Mom or Dad?

"Griffin!" it came again. Definitely not Dad.

"Griffin!" Not Mom, either.

"Laila! Is that you? Where are you? I'm . . . I don't know where I am. In a cell somewhere. Are you in a cell? Are you close? What happened to you?"

"Griffin!" Laila's voice rang twice as loud among the cells. "Stop talking. I'm here. Somewhere. Within extra-loud shouting distance of you, at least."

"That's great!" The adrenaline pulse of joy that shot through Griffin at hearing Laila's voice felt like it could flatten the entire Forge in a puff of white fog. They shouted to each other until their throats hurt. And for the first time Griffin drifted to sleep in the uncomfortable cell with a smile on his face. Laila was safe. She was nearby. All he had to do was shout to hear her voice. He could take on the entire painground and every Merciless in the Forge now.

From that point on, every morning when he woke up, he would yell her name. And every morning when she woke up, she would yell his name. And before they went to sleep. And whenever they were lonely or scared or hurting, which was all the time.

Every day, Laila would shout, "Do you still love reptiles? Do you dream about feeding hunks of meat to crocodiles?" And Griffin would shout back, "Yes, I do. Do you still love the stars? Do you dream about making footprints on Mars?" And Laila would shout, "Yes, I do."

And they would shout this mantra and other encouragement despite boos and yells and shouts for them to stop, to shut off that noise, to quiet down, by all their schoolmates in the cells around them. It was like they were surrounded by a crowd of adults. And then there were times when Laila and Griffin's shouts turned to screams when the Merciless came for them.

Eventually, by what he estimated to be the twenty-fifth cycle of painground and cell, Griffin ripped his ragged yellow cast off. His arm felt okay. Or at least the pain he felt there wasn't any worse than the pain in the rest of his body. The arm looked sickeningly thin and weak from dis-use, shriveled to almost bone, the skin pale and flaky. It felt like he could break it again just by squeezing his fist.

And then, somewhere around the thirtieth cycle, his hair longer, his weight down, his clothes shredded, but his eyes still lizard-bright thanks to Laila, he was awoken from a sleep full of nightmares to see a face at the bars of his cell. That happened every day. Whenever it was time to go to the painground. But this time, it wasn't the cold boulder and cones of a Merciless. It was the soft, warm, nubby fea-tures of a human being.

CHAPTER 32

Smashed into White Dust

The roguish countenance peering at him behind stripes of iron was met with an expression of deep-down relief from Griffin. "Ozzie!" he shouted.

"Shhhh!" Ozzie waved both of his hands over his face like he had been the one who shouted. "I'm here to rescue you," he said.

"How?" Griffin whispered.

"Oh, wait. Sorry, wrong cell. Not you." Ozzie's head disappeared, but then reappeared three seconds later. "Just kidding. Let's get you out of here."

"Help Laila," said Griffin.

"I'll get her out, too. But I found you first. Good thing you snore." He held up two severed eye-cones to his own eyes and snarled his mouth, and then took the plucked eye-cones and scratched them across the surface. It took a few tries, but finally the door clicked and opened. Ozzie raised two fists in the air and stifled the *Yes!* that tried to escape his lips. "You don't know how much I practiced getting this door unlocked." He helped Griffin out of the cell. "Nice underwear."

Griffin looked down at the shreds of his pants and saw the green lizards rampant on a field of yellow. "I left my mashed-potato monster boxers back home. Let's get Laila."

"Where is she?"

"She's . . ." Griffin realized that even though he shouted to her every day until his throat hurt, he had no clue, so he did the only thing he knew to do to find her. "Do you still love the stars?" he shouted. "Do you dream about making footprints on Mars?"

"What are you—" started Ozzie. Griffin hushed him this time.

A weak voice wafted across the cells, "Yes, I do."

"Laila!" said Ozzie. He ran toward the voice, Griffin behind, listening to her continue the questions and making sure he answered as he tried to keep up with Ozzie. They had never left that mantra unfinished in their entire lives.

Ozzie found her cell quickly, and then set about scratching at the door with the eye-cones. She looked as bad as Griffin felt. Her clothes were ripped and her legs were wobbly and she had the dazed look of someone who

190

had just gone through a marathon nightmare.

"Where's your cast?" she asked. "How long have we been here?"

Griffin shrugged and turned to Ozzie. Ozzie shrugged, too. "How in the world do you tell time in this place?" Ozzie asked.

"It felt like forever," said Laila.

"What took you so long?" asked Griffin.

"Let's get to a safe spot and I'll tell you."

They didn't have to discuss the safe spot. The three quietly crept through the labyrinth of cells until they made it through an opening in the wall and up a ladder, where they settled into the ceiling guts of the Forge.

"It was obvious pretty fast that the plan failed," said Ozzie, sitting on a dark beam, his legs dangling from it like he was on a pier. "Those squid stones really messed up everything."

"Squid stones," said Griffin. "Those things with the tentacles that cratered the ground?"

"Yeah. You guys had no chance of sneaking in with those things whistling and booming outside. Man, Leech was so mad. It spit spikes and almost punched the fang rocks we were hiding in into rubble. It was kind of endearing." He clicked his teeth together, imitating the fangs of the Merciless. "We went back to the stone cabin to regroup.

We didn't know if the Forge Merciless suspected Leech's rebels were behind your return or if you told them about us. Not that I'd blame you if you did . . ."

"We didn't," said Laila, stretching her arms on a length of piping above her head. She didn't even have to check with Griffin before speaking for both of them.

"That's what we eventually figured, too, when the Forge Merciless didn't send out any search parties. Then we had to wait for the squid stones to get cleared and the ground to get repaired. Apparently, squid stones are a real nuisance here."

"Everything's a real nuisance here," said Griffin.

"Yeah. There were like dozens of them out there in front of the Forge. I hid in one of the rock outcroppings and watched the Forge Merciless try to get rid of them with their hand Glares. It took a long time, and I saw two of the Merciless bite it badly while they were doing it. Smashed into white dust by those things." He shivered and looked down through the ceiling guts at the metal floor below.

"And then Leech wouldn't let us try again until we had a Plan B, a Plan C, a Plan D, everything through Plan Z. I was their last shot. And we had to abort a few times. Even after the squid stones were cleared, the Forge Merciless posted guards to make sure they got them all. Today, we tried again, and I made it across the plain and through the Glare to turn it off." His voice faltered at the word *Glare*. "The whole thing was like a video game. Our first two lives didn't get far, but we learned enough so that the third life could succeed. That's me. The third life. The one we win the game on."

Our first two lives. Griffin looked over at Laila. "I never thanked you for saving me from the squid stones."

Laila nodded. "Good thing I was already following you. I couldn't let you go through the Glare alone."

"I hate that you did that," said Griffin, holding a hand up before she could interrupt. "But I couldn't have gotten through the painground without you." Griffin waited for Ozzie to make fun of them, but he didn't. He chewed on his lip and stared off into the ceiling guts, no doubt remembering Desda.

"Should we find Desda and let all the other kids out?" asked Griffin.

"I tried. She just slammed the door back shut on herself." Ozzie looked down at the space below them again. "But there's really no reason to let anybody else out yet. Once Leech and the rebels take the control center of the Forge, we'll be able to do it easily. But I couldn't let you two stay in your cells any longer than I had to."

"So what do we do?" asked Laila.

"Leech said we should hang tight until we hear from them," said Ozzie.

"It said those words?" asked Griffin. "Hang tight?"

"Well, no, it was more like"—Ozzie lowered his voice and made it raspy—"'Stay in the rafters, soft child, until I come for you.'"

"No way we're hanging tight," said Laila.

"Yeah, no way," said Griffin. "Hanging tight is what we've been doing all this time."

Ozzie smiled big. "Good, because I had no intention of waiting for Leech, either. It has its own reasons for wanting to shut this place down and couldn't really care less about us. We need to make sure it lets everybody out and gets us all home. We just need to find the control center. And, hopefully, by the time we do, Leech will have control over it."

"Do you know where the control center is?" asked Laila.

"Somewhere . . . ," said Ozzie, moving one of his hands in circular motion to indicate the area below them, "down there."

"Great," said Laila.

The three started moving through the ceiling guts like frilled lizards in a rain-forest canopy. It was slow going, sometimes more vertical than horizontal as they climbed around shafts and across platforms and around tracks. Also, Laila and Griffin weren't in the best form after a month alternating between being cramped in a cell and tormented on the painground. Especially Griffin. He found it harder to climb and crawl with a weak arm than with an encased one. The arm felt like it was going to snap in half if he put too much of his meager weight on it. A few times they made wrong turns and ended up back above the painground. They found themselves above rooms they couldn't identify, some so awash in white fog it was impossible to see anything below, as well as above solid ceilings that hid the purposes of the rooms. Griffin worried that maybe one of those hidden rooms was the control center, which meant they would never find it from up in the ceiling. It also occurred to Griffin that he had no idea what a control center looked like. He had a vague notion of a room with lots of those black control tables, maybe a bunch of screens on the walls.

And then they found a room with a bunch of those black control tables and screens on the walls. And what they saw in that room made their stomachs drop.

CHAPTER 33

I Suck at Dodgeball

Despite the dimness of the room, Griffin could see Leech's rebels. He recognized their metal-studded heads as they peeked from the barred windows of a bank of black cells off to the side of the room.

"They failed. They've all been captured," Laila whispered.

"We need to restart the game," Griffin whispered back.

The control room looked like the interior of a black cube. The walls and floor were covered in Black Slide leather, with metal rivets making dotted lines throughout. A metal dais against one wall featured banks of invisible controls. There were about a dozen Merciless at those controls, plus a half dozen more guarding the cells.

The Merciless scraped their eye-cones and fingertips on the walls and control banks. Video screens of various

196

sizes flashed on the walls. The feeds on the screens looked glitchy, all the light parts dark and all the dark parts light like there was a negative filter over the screens. Some showed the torment of the painground. Others zoomed in on the agony of a single kid. Other screens showed what looked like charts and graphs of a peculiar geometry. One large screen above them all revealed a glowing line emanating at an angle from a rectangular shape surrounded by flickering characters that must have been the written language of the Merciless.

"Look," said Griffin, pointing to that screen. "That must be the Black Slide." Griffin wondered what more the Merciless were seeing on the screens through the alternate vision of their eye-cones.

"We have to free Leech and the rebels," said Laila.

"How?" asked Griffin.

"Ozzie knows how to open those things," said Laila, pointing at the bank of cells. Ozzie held up the severed eye-cones like he'd found spare change in his pocket. "So we have to get him over there."

Griffin counted the number of Forge Merciless again but stopped when he saw some carrying discs in their hands. "They have hand Glares."

"We'll have to not get hit," said Ozzie. "Like in dodge-ball."

"I suck at dodgeball," said Griffin.

"It'll be more like capture the flag," said Laila. "Distracting the other team and sneaking around." She looked down at the control center. "Two doorways. One there"— she pointed at the far end of the room near the cells—"and one there." That one was across the room from the other doorway, closer to the dais. "We can do this." She led them through the guts of the ceiling away from the control center until they were less exposed. Then she laid out a plan. It was a good one, and Griffin absolutely hated it.

"We have to find a way to the far door of the control room. The one near the cells," said Laila.

Ozzie gave her two thumbs up and a silly grin. "Follow me." He took off through the ceiling guts. He kept the control center on his left as he tried to circle around to the doorway they had seen by the cells. Even so, they had to try three different ladders before they found the right one. Griffin's weak arm was starting to hurt.

They were in a small chamber that connected two larger rooms. They stayed flattened against the wall, while Laila stuck a fraction of her face around the corner. She pulled it back in. "I say we run all the way to the dais and get the attention of as many as we can along the way. Then, when we get to the dais, we pivot hard and run out that far door. Hopefully we'll get chased and clear out the room enough. And hopefully Ozzie can free Leech and the others. And then hopefully they can take care of everything so that Griffin and me getting caught won't mean anything."

"There are a lot of hopefullys in this plan," said Ozzie.

"I'm full of hope," said Laila. She turned and looked at Griffin. "Do you still love reptiles? Do you dream about feeding hunks of meat to crocodiles?"

"Yes, I do," said Griffin. "Do you still love the stars? Do you dream about making footprints on Mars?"

"Yes, I do," said Laila.

"You two are weird," said Ozzie.

And with that send-off, Laila and Griffin ran into a room full of armed Merciless like they were racing to be first in line at an ice cream truck.

CHAPTER 34

Last One Out Gets
a Choker around Their Neck

In fourth grade, Griffin had played George Washington in the school play. He'd had to wear a white wig and white socks up to his knees and a jacket with lots of brass-colored buttons. He hated it. He didn't like the costume. He didn't like being onstage. He didn't like being the center of attention. He didn't like the way his dad made fun of him about the play, even though he didn't come to see it. But Griffin knew he had to give the best George Washington that he could, even if his best was terrible. That was the only way to make it through the play with the least amount of suffering. Giving his all and being embarrassed was much better than not giving his all and being embarrassed. Giving his all distracted him from some of the misery.

So Griffin gave his all this time. And it kind of felt like

a play, too. Like he wasn't Griffin Birch in this moment, but an actor playing a character who looked like Griffin Birch, from his stick arm all the way down to his reptile underwear.

"Hello, Merciless!" said Griffin as loud as he could. White globes with shiny points spun at him from around the room. "I'm Griffin Birch. I'm here for the tour of the control room!"

"And I'm Laila Brooks!" said Laila, following his lead. She had skirted by the fourth-grade play with only a small role in the Constitutional Convention scene. "I've been looking forward to this field trip all year. And here I am, finally getting to see the pain center of a Forge. Unbelievable." Maybe she should have played George Washington.

"And what do you do here?" Griffin asked a Merciless with large metal rings embedded in each side of its head. It was standing by a wall screen that showed a squid stone blinking its empty white eyes. The Merciless didn't respond, just kept flicking its eye-cones between the screen and Griffin. "You're too busy to talk; I understand," said Griffin. "Important work going on here. Keep it up!" He slapped the Merciless on the back and instantly regretted it as his hand stung all the way to his elbow like he had smacked a cinder block.

Laila was squeaking her hand across one of the black

walls. "What is this remarkable stuff? I need this for my bedroom."

Griffin and Laila kept talking, aware that nobody was chasing them yet or pulling out their weapons. Griffin couldn't read any emotions on the faces of the Merciless, but he assumed they were too surprised and confused to act. He and Laila were so successful at being the center of attention in the control center that it was only Griffin who glimpsed Ozzie slipping into the room and hiding behind one of the cells. Now all Griffin and Laila had to do was lead as many of the Merciless away as possible. An entire nightmare of Merciless is how Griffin thought of them as a group—the way a group of alligators is called a congregation and a group of turtles is a bale.

But if the Merciless were feeling too surprised or confused to act at first, that soon ended. No Merciless drew their hand Glares, but somehow, many of them suddenly had choker poles in their fists, the studded loops quivering at the ends, hungry for the necks of soft children.

"I think our field trip is over," said Griffin.

"Last one out gets a choker around their neck," said Laila. She sped across the room and out the door that was away from the cells and Ozzie.

Griffin was soon behind her, running as fast as his legs would take him and for some reason feeling like he was slower without a cast slamming his rib cage. With Laila in front, he didn't have to worry about where they were heading, as long as he kept her in his sights. She was the one who needed to worry about where they were going. If this had been a real chase, it would be up the first ladder they saw. But they didn't want to lose the Merciless chasing them. They wanted to distract the Merciless for as long as possible.

They ran down a corridor that seemed as long as the Forge itself. They could feel the heavy footsteps of the Merciless behind them vibrating the floor, hear the gravelly grunts and high-pitched shrieks as the Merciless screamed who-knew-what after them. Griffin didn't dare turn around. Not that he would have seen them. Outside the control center, the fog started thickening in the already dark hallway, making it hard to follow Laila and turning what was gaining on them with choker poles in their hands even more terrifying. Griffin swore he'd had this nightmare before. A million times before. Being chased through dark, foggy hallways with an unseen menace growling and screaming and clacking sharp teeth behind him. Everybody had that nightmare.

The corridor turned and ended at a doorway, which they sped through into a small room with a ladder. Griffin looked longingly at it as he followed Laila through another opening and down another long, fog-filled corridor. Laila took random doorways into random rooms, and Griffin struggled to keep up. Eventually, one of the doorways opened onto the dark haunted-house roller rink of the painground. They heard the screams of their classmates, the buzzing and flashing of Glare weapons. Laila took off at a sprint through the dense white fog, weaving around painground equipment and putting even more distance between her and Griffin. He didn't know what he was more scared of, getting separated from her or getting caught by the Merciless.

At the far side of the painground was another opening, just visible through a break in the fog. But to get there, they didn't just have to outrun the Merciless behind them. They had to evade the Merciless who tended the painground. Griffin tried not to look around at the kids strapped to the equipment. He kept his eyeballs on Laila's back, just like in class when he was trying not to stare out the window at the playground.

By the time he took another twenty steps, discombobulated by the lights and the fog, Griffin realized he didn't need to worry about where they were going anymore. He saw the flash of metal-studded black drop across his eyes almost after he felt it constrict around his neck.

CHAPTER 35

I'll Knock You through the Rings of Saturn

Being caught in the choker was almost as big a relief as exiting the Glare. Griffin had done his part. He'd acted in the play. He'd given it his all. He'd done everything he could possibly do for this plan. He'd done more than that. He'd gone down the Black Slide. Escaped the cells. Escaped the Forge. Survived the metal plain and all its monsters. Found his way back into the Forge. Now all he needed to do was get captured. That's it. To give in. The studded loop around his neck meant that everything was out of his hands but still on the right track. And that was an amazing feeling.

Laila seemed less euphoric about the loop around her neck. Three loops, actually. "Get these off me, you moonheads!" Three Merciless were trying to pull her toward where Griffin was being held by only one Merciless, but she was putting up a fight. Not a desperate "You'll never take me alive" type of fight. An "I'm not going to make this easy for you" type of fight. "I swear I'll knock you through the rings of Saturn," she yelled.

Standing there with a choker around his neck and surrounded by the Merciless in the middle of a painground, Griffin smiled. Laila was the only reason that he had been able to withstand everything so far. He could take on anything as long as she was around.

The building shuddered like it was a block of Jell-O, and a piece of metal piping fell from the high-above ceiling to the floor with a crash. Griffin revised what he thought he could take. He looked at the Merciless to see if he could read anything on their faces, but of course he couldn't. They grumbled and shrieked to each other like they were arguing among themselves, but that was always how they talked to each other. Two of them got close enough that the tips of their eye-cones touched.

"What's happening?" Griffin asked Laila, and then he gagged when his question was rewarded with a harsh tug on the choker. Laila shrugged her shoulders. "Maybe Leech is doing his thing?" Her voice was raspy from the chokers around her neck.

That's right, thought Griffin. The building coming

down around them might be good news, other than the fact that the building was coming down around them. Another piece of black metal fell from the ceiling, ricocheting off the control panels in the middle of the painground.

As if the crash had been a starting bell, the nightmare of Merciless started pulling and jerking him and Laila toward the far door through which they had come. That probably meant they were going back to the control center, although Griffin couldn't be sure. He'd gotten lost in all the running down corridors and dashing through rooms. As they walked, the building stopped shaking.

Soon his suspicion was confirmed when the Merciless led them into the black cube, where they were immediately accosted by other Merciless.

Actually, it was the Merciless that led them into the control room that were accosted. Four Merciless wearing sashes crackled hand Glares at them. Griffen cringed and threw his hands up, but no pain came. He opened his eyes to see the rebel Merciless dragging the limp Forge Merciless away, leaving Laila and Griffin by themselves with choker poles dangling from their necks.

Leech stood on the dais. He had also removed the vertical strip of black material from his chest and replaced it with a sash. Elsewhere, Merciless in shiny strips were being taken to the bank of black cells, the number of which was growing as more were dropped off via a track in the ceiling.

"We did it!" said Laila. "It worked." She pulled the chokers off her head and threw them to the ground, where they fell to the black leather floor with a dull clatter.

Leech had taken over the control room. Shark Fin Head and Buzzsaw Head and Checkerboard Head and the rest were either stuffing Forge Merciless into cells or were busy scratching at the control panels and screens with their fingers and eye-cones.

"Do you see Ozzie?" Griffin asked Laila, removing the choker from his own neck and dropping it to thud on the floor.

"No," said Laila.

"Leech!" Griffin yelled up at the Merciless. "Where's Ozzie?"

Leech looked at Griffin for the first time since they'd entered, screeched something to the room, and all new chokers were placed around their necks from behind. It all happened so quickly and was such a surprise that Griffin and Laila didn't even flinch.

"What's happening? Why are you doing this?" shouted Griffin to Leech as they were pulled toward the cells. Laila shouted similar questions at the metal-veined Merciless. Except she used "moon-head" a lot. Leech didn't respond.

It just went back to one of the control panels on the dais while spitting orders at the other Merciless.

"We were used," said a voice deep within the block of cells, no metallic scrapes or rocky grumbles in its tone, just pure human defeat. Ozzie's face appeared in the barred window, and the Forge started to rumble and shake again.

CHAPTER 36

Everyone's a Bad Guy

Unlike the Merciless at the painground, these Merciless didn't seem to notice that the building was shaking. They stuffed Griffin and Laila into cells beside Ozzie's and walked away. When the building stopped rumbling, Ozzie said, "Sorry I couldn't warn you. They were holding a Glare on me."

"Your screams of pain would have warned us," said Laila.

"You sound like a Merciless," said Ozzie.

"What happened?" asked Griffin.

"I snuck to the cells and unlocked Leech, like I was supposed to. Once we'd freed all the rebels, it was Glare weapons everywhere. A real laser-gun fight. And ferocious. The Merciless don't mess around."

"I thought the Merciless like the Glare," said Laila.

"Or at least the ones without holes in their chests."

"I don't know if they like it," said Ozzie. "Or if they just believe in it. But it does knock them out of the action for a bit, which is awkward in a fight. Leech wasn't lying about the Glare, though. It hurts the rebels bad. One zap, and they were on the floor, completely out of it. Anyway, I hid behind the cells and stayed out of the way. But the rebels won quickly since you'd thinned out the Forge Merciless so much. After Leech took control, they brought in more cells, loaded them up with prisoners, and then threw me in, too, after taking my eye-cones. It was embarrassing."

"That doesn't sound embarrassing. That sounds infuriating," said Laila.

"Well, I was trying to give Leech a high five at the time. It left me hanging, said something about a Black Tunnel, and then it was back to talking like an engine full of bricks and I was in a cell."

"What have we done?" asked Griffin.

"Everyone's a bad guy in the Painful Place," said Laila.

The building rumbled again, stopping the conversation. Griffin waited for the ceiling guts to fall on them. When the rumbling stopped, he said, "At least it sounds like Leech is destroying the Black Slide. Even if we don't get home, that's something."

"Yup, something," said Laila, although the way she said

it sounded like her something meant something different from Griffin's something.

Griffin looked at the glowing schematic of the Black Slide on the wall. The Black Slide looked bigger for some reason. And when the Forge shook and rumbled again, he watched it grow even more.

"Leech didn't tell you anything else about what the rebels are planning to do?" asked Griffin.

Ozzie didn't answer.

"Ozzie?"

Nothing.

"Ozzie!"

"Sorry, I'm a little busy," said Ozzie.

"What could you possibly be busy doing in that tiny cell?" asked Griffin.

"Trying to figure out how this works." His hand snaked out between the bars, and Griffin could see it holding a disc with finger holes.

"How'd you get a Glare weapon?" asked Laila.

"During the fight. Pulled it off a Merciless on the floor."

"What are you going to do with it?" asked Griffin.

"As soon as I figure out how to use it, I'm going to threaten one of the rebel Merciless with it until it opens our cells." He pulled the hand Glare back inside and

212

Griffin could hear him fiddling with it. "I wish this thing were shaped like a regular gun with a big ol' trigger on it. Would make it a lot easier."

"Be careful," said Laila. "You might shoot your—"

Griffin heard spritzy feedback, saw Ozzie's window glow red, and then heard a scream echo from the cell. "Ozzie! Are you okay?" Ozzie didn't answer.

"Ozzie! Ozzie, can you hear us?" shouted Laila.

They heard a groan from the depths of his cell that eventually resolved into words. "I'm okay. And I've got good news. I know which way to point this thing." There were two seconds of silence after his statement, and then Griffin and Laila laughed—short, bright, unexpected sounds that were quickly doused in those black cells. Griffin saw a Merciless across the room aim its eye-cones at them briefly and then turn away.

"Now we need to get one of them over here," said Griffin.

"Hey, metal-mouths! Come here!" yelled Ozzie.

"Moon-heads, we've got something to show you!" shouted Laila.

"Over here, uhhhhhh, guys!" yelled Griffin.

But no matter how much they shouted and insulted and screamed their lungs through their mouths, not a single Merciless even looked at them. The screams of kids

were commonplace for them, like the hum of a refriger-
ator. They probably liked it. Listened to it at their homes
when they weren't working at the Forge to set the mood.
Played it at parties. The three of them weren't going to lure
any Merciless with their shouts and screams.

The Forge rumbled and shook again, and Griffin
braced himself against the sides of the cell, grateful that
he had both arms again. As the noise and vibrations died
down, Griffin remembered the Merciless who had looked
at them before they had started shouting. When Laila and
he made sounds it might never have heard before, that
would never happen on a painground, that would never
come out of the experiments.

Griffin looked down and started cracking up.

"Griffin's lost it," said Ozzie.

"My pants," Griffin managed between guffaws.
"They've been ripped, shredded, dissolved, worn through.
I'm almost in my underwear here." He kept laughing.

"They have little green lizards on them," said Ozzie, a
chuckle in his throat expanding into a full-blown guffaw.

"And they're yellow," said Laila, contracting the con-
tagious laughter from the other two. "They matched your
cast. You matched your arm cast to your underwear!"

"I might as well have worn a clown suit!" said Griffin,
breathless from all the giggling.

"A clown in the Painful Place!" laughed Ozzie.

"Ronald McDonald sitting in a cage tree!" howled Laila.

"Perched on a mound monster!" roared Griffin.

They laughed and laughed and invented even more ridiculous scenarios and it felt good, so they laughed some more—and soon, one of the Merciless walked over to see what the alien-sounding commotion was. It was the one they called Liberty Head because of its arc of spikes bisecting its head from temple to temple like the crown on the Statue of Liberty. Ozzie was laughing so hard and so sincerely that he forgot to brandish the hand Glare until Griffin shouted at him.

Ozzie's laughter ended like he'd been choked as he shoved the hand Glare through the bars. It crackled and fuzzed ominously. "I'll shoot your insides full of red pain if you don't let me out right now."

The Merciless might or might not have understood English, but it definitely understood a Glare pointed at it. It scratched the place on its chest where the hole was and then scratched its eyes across the door of Ozzie's cell until it popped open. Ozzie made the Merciless open Griffin's and Laila's cells and then shut it inside one they had emptied.

"Now what?" asked Griffin.

"We slip out through that door, get to the ceiling guts," said Ozzie.

215

"Or we could give up," said Laila.

Griffin turned, confused at her dismal remark, but quickly understood. They were surrounded by a nightmare of Merciless, all wielding staticky-sounding Glares.

It had been a short jailbreak.

CHAPTER 37

How You Doomed Your World

Griffin steeled himself for the flare of red pain and inched back toward the cells. He could see Laila and Ozzie doing the same on both sides of him, Ozzie with his hands up, letting the hand Glare dangle from his fingers in a way that was supposed to look unthreatening.

He was so anticipating the agony that he barely heard the scream of a Merciless sear the air from the direction of the dais. The Merciless surrounding them heard it, though. They immediately turned and ran without so much as a sneer at the three of them.

"Where are they going?" asked Ozzie, putting his hands down and carefully readjusting his grip on the weapon.

"Looks like this place is about to turn into a battle-ground again," said Griffin. Merciless poured into the

217

control room, all of them wearing vertical strips of shiny black. The Forge shook and groaned again, causing the Merciless to stumble and thud into each other as they ran into the chaos that was filling the room.

"Is that Gutter?" asked Laila, pointing to the far doorway.

Griffin had almost forgotten about the bald Merciless. But there it was, or one that looked like it, fighting with a ferocity that was even more terrifying than when Griffin had first seen it on the playground back home.

"We . . . should escape, right?" said Ozzie.

"I'd definitely feel a lot more comfortable in the ceiling," said Griffin. Flashes of red lit up the room to the loud soundtrack of distortion feedback.

Griffin, Ozzie, and Laila fled through the back entrance and scampered up the ladder like frightened squirrels. It took them a few minutes to clamber back to their previous vantage point, and when they did, they were greeted by a horrible tableau of violence. Red flashes lit the room like explosions and the air was full of Glare noise and screams and shouts like cracking mountains and falling skyscrapers. Some of the Merciless had black shields that seemed to deflect the Glare. Others had thick black cudgels studded with metal spikes for closer combat.

Hunks and powder trails of white Merciless flesh lay

scattered across the black floor, dug out by spiky cudgels and sharp metal-tipped fingers.

"For creatures obsessed with immortality, they don't mind destroying each other," said Laila, watching a Merciless with coils of metal springing out of its head salting the floor with the face of a Merciless with a metal bowl on its head.

Still, there was a strange sort of dance to the combat. Like every Merciless in the room wanted to both win and lose. Like giving a club to the head was as good as getting one. Like a scream of agony was in the same key as a scream of victory. Griffin still didn't understand this strange race, not even a little bit, but this battle might have been his best view of it so far.

"This is awful," said Laila.

"Could be worse," said Griffin. "At least they're made of rock. Better than if the place was covered in blood and guts."

"Who are we even rooting for?" asked Ozzie.

As the Merciless fought each other, the Forge shook and rumbled intermittently, each time almost dislodging the three from their perches high above the frenzy.

Griffin looked at the glowing, pulsing schematic of the Black Slide on the wall. The angled line at the top of the Forge had grown even thicker. His attention was quickly pulled away, though, as more Merciless poured into the control center, grinding and screeching at the top of their ossified lungs, all of them with vertical strips dangling from their necks. It became clear quickly that the Forge Merciless outnumbered the rebels and were winning.

And then it became terribly, horrifically clear that they had won.

Gutter stood as still as a stone pyre on the dais while around it other Forge Merciless feverishly worked their eye-cones and fingertips on the control panels. Gutter's eye-cones were pointed directly at the space in front of the dais, where two Merciless held chokers around Leech's neck.

Gutter stepped off the dais and squared up to the metal-veined Leech, close enough that their eye-cones touched. Gutter waved at the other two Merciless, who removed their chokers and walked away.

Gutter screech-grated something to Leech, who remained silent as stone and unmoved as bedrock. Gutter held out a hand to the side, and a spiky cudgel was immediately placed in it by a nearby Merciless. Gutter smashed Leech in the side of the head with it, quickly, forcefully, and then followed it up with another strike from the other direction. Specks of white flew off Leech's head like broken human teeth. Gutter dropped the cudgel to the floor and reached out toward Leech. It ripped open the sash and robe of the rebel, revealing its pale, metal-embedded chest and the dark hole in its center. Gutter pulled a hand Glare out of its own robes and placed it point-blank against the hole in Leech's chest. The sound of static erupted and Leech was suffused with red, its head-veins and eye-cones and teeth glowing like lava. The white stone of its flesh burned like a red cinder. Leech collapsed to its knees, and then fell forward, smashing its face on the floor with a sound like a dropped cantaloupe. Gutter lifted its boot and stomped Leech's head into a pile of flour.

Ozzie screamed, and Laila threw her hand over her mouth, and Griffin grabbed desperately at a length of beam for support. Every eye-cone in the control center suddenly pointed at them. Including Gutter's.

It stood above Leech's remains, a small evil smile wounding its face and displaying its black hole full of metal shark fins. "Come down, soft children," it said. "Come see how you doomed your world."

CHAPTER 38

None of This Matters, Right?

"What do we do?" whispered Laila, like the entire room of Merciless wasn't staring up at them.

"We go down, I think," said Griffin.

"What are you talking about?" asked Ozzie, staring down at Gutter like he was waiting for it to sprout bat wings and fly up to get them.

Griffin felt inevitability settle on him like snow. "We've been trying to escape this place for who knows how long, and every time it feels like we've escaped, we end up worse off. I'm tired of it. Tired of trying, tired of hoping, tired of running, tired of being scared. We should just go down. Stop fighting whatever's happening."

"I don't want to be experimented on," said Ozzie.

"What?" said Griffin. "You've been trying to convince us to be like Desda since we got here."

222

"I've changed my mind."

"I've never changed mine," said Laila. "I don't want to be experimented on anymore either."

"It's going to happen anyway, right?" said Griffin. "Like Leech said? Our world will harden us even if we weren't experimented on by the Merciless. Parents and teachers and bullies and . . . and . . . and just life. Pain and disappointment and loss. I don't know. Maybe we're the lucky ones. The experiments will speed up the process. But one thing is for sure. There's only one way back. Through the Black Slide."

The building started to rumble again, almost knocking them out of the ceiling guts, and Griffin glanced over at the schematic. The thick bar got thicker. "I don't think it's any safer up here than it is down there, anyway," he said.

A grinding shriek below reminded them that they had an audience.

"We'll follow you," said Laila. Ozzie nodded.

The three crawled through the ceiling guts and back to the ladder. They expected chokers the second they set foot in the control center, but the Merciless ignored them, going about the business of locking up what was left of the rebels, cleaning up the bodies and chunks off the floor, and monitoring screens and control panels. As they neared the dais, Gutter welcomed them with a flesh-eating grin.

"Soft children, you have been trouble from the start. But it was always just trouble for us and trouble for you. Now you have made trouble for your home."

"What does our home have to do with this?" asked Griffin.

"The rebels disagree with how we use your world," said Gutter.

"We know," said Ozzie. "We've heard this story."

"You heard lies," said Gutter. "The rebels believe we are too conservative with our methods. They want us to conquer your world instead of experimenting on such a small sample. To transform it. Cover its softness with metal and stone. Scour it down to bedrock. Enslave your entire soft population for the experiments."

Things only ever get worse here, thought Griffin.

"But to do that, they would need to get an army through the Black Slide. And that is impossible." Gutter bent over and dragged its eyes across a control panel, and the Black Slide schematic on the wall expanded and took on more details.

"Black Tunnel," said Ozzie. "Leech was talking about a Black Tunnel."

Griffin looked at the thick bar atop the Forge, a massive tunnel into the sky. The building rumbled and the Black Slide got bigger. He finally realized what was happening.

"They were expanding the Black Slide," he said. "Turning it into a Black Tunnel big enough to fit an army."

"But none of this matters, right?" said Laila. "The rebels are powder." She scraped at a stray bit of white dust with her shoe, but then grimaced and stopped when she realized what she was scraping at.

"We defeated their raiding party." Gutter scratched the control panel with three fingers. The schematic on the wall shrank, and beside it appeared an image that was difficult to make out due to the inverted black and white. "Look."

"I can't see anything." said Griffin.

"Useless eye-spheres," Gutter rumbled and then bent and poked at a control panel with its eye-cones. The screen resolved into a clearer view of the metal plain behind the Forge. Humps of mound monsters were scattered across the riveted surface, almost glowing in the eerie cloud light. At first, it was difficult to see what was different about the view. But then movement on the dark horizon revealed a writhing mass coating it. Gutter scratched the controls again, and the screen zoomed in on the mass.

It was an army. Thousands of Merciless marching toward them. A black tide of metal and stone headed for the Forge.

CHAPTER 39

They Will Torture Your World into a Higher Existence

Griffin needed a new word to describe a group of Merciless. *Nightmare* wasn't strong enough for what he saw seething across the metal plain, eye-cones aimed in the same direction, black mouths writhing around metal teeth, black robes shimmering below ghostly white orbs. He remembered how Leech had told them it had three thousand rebels, and then retracted the number, blaming it on its grasp of English. But maybe Leech had slipped and spoken the truth and then lied to cover up its plan to create the Black Tunnel to invade Earth. Griffin was so distracted by the thought that he almost missed that the Merciless weren't alone.

"What in the Painful Place are those things?" asked Laila, beating him to the question.

They were giants. Twenty times the size of the tiny

Merciless figures surging around their feet, maybe ninety or a hundred feet tall. They looked like they were made of ice or crystal, faceted like gemstones but completely transparent. The features of their faces were like the furrows and jags of an iceberg, and inside their torsos was a complex arrangement of brightly colored shapes, like their internal organs were massive jewels. Those organs pulsed colored light that illuminated their bodies in the dark. One of the giants pushed a pair of screaming clouds out of its way like a bunch of annoying party balloons while another flattened a clutch of mound monsters with its foot.

And Griffen recognized them. He had seen the head of one of these giants, glinting on the horizon as a false dawn when they had first escaped the Forge. It chilled him to think they could have run into one of those titans out on the seamed, riveted plains. It terrified him to know they were bearing down on the Forge now. But they were beautiful. Beautiful in a way nothing in the Painful Place was. Or they would be if they weren't ankle deep in an ugly Merciless army.

"Diants," said Gutter. "I do not know how the rebels got them to join, but they are a big problem for us."

"Can't you stop all this?" asked Griffin, panic creeping up through his body like a choking vine. "You've got the control center. Just turn off the Black Tunnel."

"I can do that," said Gutter. "But it takes time, and the rest of the Opened Ones will be here too soon."

"The Opened Ones?" asked Laila.

Gutter stuck a sharp finger in its chest and traced a small circle, like the hole they had seen in Leech's chest. Griffin still couldn't read the cold white expressions of the Merciless, but it was almost like Gutter was enjoying the situation. Maybe it was. After all, its world wasn't in danger.

"Doesn't this place have weapons? Defenses? Something to protect the Forge?" asked Griffin.

"Before you soft children snuck the rebels inside?" Gutter waited until it received a reluctant yes from all three of them before continuing. "Yes. The Glare protects us from the Opened Ones. And not only the doorways. When threatened, the Forge can deliver a field of solid Glare extending far beyond these walls and across the plains surrounding us. The Opened Ones would suffer immediate death. We do not know if it hurts the Diants, but they generally ignore us."

"Do that, then," said Ozzie. "Like, quickly."

"We cannot. Leech sabotaged the controls. We are defenseless. The Opened Ones will come, they will take over the Forge, they will march through the Black Tunnel, and they will torture your world into a higher existence as they try to wring every bit of data out of you to help the Merciless become immortal." Gutter's eye-cones roved around the room before finally resting on Griffin. "Unless you commit the most excruciating act of your entire soft life."

The Forge rumbled and shook around them.

CHAPTER 40

They Come Out Dead?

Griffin didn't need to wait for the Forge to settle down to decide on his answer to Gutter's strange offer. He knew it immediately. Because whatever Gutter was talking about, it was wrong. Griffin had opened the Black Slide, broken his arm, walked through the Glare, been eaten by both a cage tree and a mound monster, walked through the Glare again, been subjected to a painground and a tiny cell, been betrayed, and watched his best friend undergo all that same torment. And then there was his pain back on Earth. Cruelty at both school and home. Abandonment by his dad. Watching his mother shrink into another person as she withdrew more into herself after dad left. His menu of agonies was long and varied—nothing could be worse than what he'd already experienced.

But he wasn't the only one who had an answer ready.

"Let's do it," said Ozzie.

"Sounds easy," said Laila.

Griffin's answer had less swagger. "Okay."

Gutter chewed its black tongue between its sharp teeth. "I am not talking to all of you. I am talking to this one." It pointed a metal-tipped finger at Griffin.

Griffin's insides collapsed into rubble in the pit of his stomach.

"Not fair," said Laila. Ozzie kept silent.

"What do I have to do?" asked Griffin.

"And *why* does he have to?" asked Laila.

Gutter scrabbled at the console until a tall panel in the wall behind the dais slid open. It was filled with a Glare that was a deeper red than any Glare Griffin had seen in the Painful Place. Blood Red, they'd call it back home. Who knew what the bloodless Merciless with their eye-cones called it.

"Through that doorway is the cortex of the Forge," said Gutter. "It is where we can reset the Glare to repel the Opened Ones and hopefully the Diants with them."

"Why don't you go through it?" said Laila. "You guys love the Glare."

"This is the highest concentration of Glare possible. No Merciless has ever experienced it and lived. That is why Leech used it to block access to the cortex."

231

"There's no other way to get in there?" asked Ozzie.

"It would take a long time for us to find a way to shut the Glare off from out here."

"Wait. If no Merciless can survive that level of Glare . . . ," started Laila.

"No human being can either," said Gutter.

"But you're asking me to," said Griffin, hoping he was wrong.

"Yes."

"Why?"

"Because you opened the Black Slide."

"I don't understand," said Griffin.

"Because you *survived* opening the Black Slide."

Griffin finally got it. "I wasn't supposed to."

"Most do not survive the opening of the Black Slide."

"They come out dead?" asked Griffin.

"They do not come out at all. But you escaped. And then you chose to go down the Black Slide again." Gutter made it sound like an accusation.

"Are you saying Griffin is special?" asked Ozzie.

"No. Lucky, perhaps. But I *am* surprised he went down the Black Slide again."

Griffin looked quickly at Laila, who gave him a tight smile and then looked away. He focused back on Gutter. "You think because I survived the Black Slide that I can take this Glare?" He nodded at the dark glow.

"I do not know. But I am interested to find out. Opening the Black Slide is an ultimate act of suffering. As is the highest level of Glare. And if you are successful, we might be able to save the Forge and your world. But that matters less to me."

Gutter was being honest with him. It wasn't trying to help them. Wasn't trying to manipulate them like Leech had done. It was giving them an option. The only option possible. An option that Griffin would take no matter what it meant. But maybe Griffin could take even more.

"I'll enter that Glare on one condition," Griffin said.

"Condition? Your world is in trouble, not mine," creaked Gutter.

"I don't think that's true," said Griffin. He was relieved that it was his turn to explain and he didn't have to listen to the ear torture of Gutter's voice. "If the Opened Ones make it through the Black Tunnel, it means everything about your work in the Forge will change. No more siphoning off a small group of children to learn the secrets of immortality. Your world will be pushed off this path. And if you believe the way to immortality lies with the Black Slide, you will never achieve it." Griffin looked directly into the sharp points of Gutter's eye-cones and tried to make his own eyes as hard as Gutter's. "Both of our worlds are in jeopardy."

"*Jeopardy's* a good word," said Laila, nodding her head.

"What is the condition?" asked Gutter.

"You send every kid in the Forge home immediately."

Gutter grumbled and gnashed its metal teeth, making sounds like a knife being sharpened. "No. Emptying the Forge is as bad as allowing the Opened Ones through the Black Tunnel. Both are soft and rotten options for me."

"It's just a bunch of fifth graders," said Griffin.

"No," Gutter said. "But I will give you this. I can free the three of you."

"We can't save everybody," said Ozzie to Griffin.

"We have to," said Laila, her eyes going liquid. "We can't leave people behind." Gutter looked away like it was disgusted or offended by her tears.

"Yeah, that's right," said Griffin. "We can't." He turned to Gutter. "So I guess that means we all just stand here and wait for the Opened Ones to get here. I think I'm actually starting to feel the steps of the Diants." He faked like the ground was shaking.

The Merciless stared at Griffin for a long while before finally making a series of harsh, sharp noises. It said, "You may have the soft children back. *If* you're successful."

CHAPTER 41

And Hope Nothing Is Going to Eat Them Today

As he stood in front of that dark ruby Glare, Griffin realized that he had done this before. He had stood in front of a dark red door, dreading what came next. The front door of his house. The last day his dad was in his life. He knew something bad was going to happen to him when he went through that red door. Knew because the front yard was littered with his broken stuff. Stuff that hadn't been broken or thrown all over the yard when he had left for school that morning. His bike was mangled. His video game console was a pile of plastic shards and circuit boards. The plush turtle that he was embarrassed for having but couldn't get rid of because it had slept in his bed since he was a baby had been shredded like a dog had got its teeth into it. But the shattered terrarium was the worst of all the litter of his life spread out in front of him.

Mom's car wasn't there. She must have had a fight with his dad. She would take off after the really bad ones. Laila was with him, and she had tried to get Griffin to go to her house, but he waved her away. He didn't want his dad to come get him there. Didn't want Laila involved in that.

Here, in front of this new and horrible red door, he could vaguely feel pressure around him and looked down to see Laila's arms. And then he saw a second pair, long and lanky, encircling her arms. Ozzie's. They both whispered something to him in the group hug that he couldn't hear. They were too far away. In a different place. A different Painful Place.

He walked up to the dark red door, awaiting more pain and maybe the end of his life. It always came back to pain. Always came back to agony. He opened it and stepped into his house. Into the Glare.

Inside his house, it had been oddly clean compared to the front yard. Nothing else in the house had been touched. The damage to Griffin's stuff hadn't been collateral. It had been the whole point. He hadn't known where to go. In his own house.

The pain in the Glare was excruciating. He balled his fists, balled his body, balled his brain, but he couldn't shrink from the hurt. He was suspended in liquid pain. Chewed up by serrated teeth. Scraped across the metal plains until his body opened. His bones burned like fire logs. His skin froze and cracked like a winter pond. His blood thickened into paste. His skull was a throbbing time bomb.

He had seen a light on in the kitchen and followed it. His dad had been leaning back against the sink, facing Griffin, a lit cigarette extended from his mouth like a small, burning tusk. He had been wearing one of his expensive work suits. The kind that if Griffin even breathed on he got smacked on the top of the head. His dad's hand had been extended over the metal basin. In his fingers, held delicately by the tail, had been Griffin's pet anole. His only pet, his first pet, his first reptile. It was four inches long and looked especially tiny and vulnerable dangling from his dad's thick fingers.

"You love this lizard, don't you?" his dad had said. "What's its name again? Lenny? Lenny the Lizard?"

His dad had known the reptile's name, but Griffin had corrected him anyway. "Liza the Lizard." The bright green lizard had twitched its pointed head back and forth, like it had recognized either its name or Griffin's voice.

"I don't like lizards," his dad had said, lifting Liza to eye level. "They don't do anything. They don't play fetch. They can't catch a mouse. They just sit very still on their branches and hope nothing is going to eat them today. A lot like you. Probably why you love it so much."

The Glare saturated him with pain. Filled every cell. Became an inseparable part of him. He was pain, and it was worse than merely feeling pain.

"I'm tired of spending money on crickets for this thing, I think," his dad had said, reaching for a switch on the wall. The garbage disposal started up with a grumbling roar and a shriek of spinning metal teeth, and his dad slowly lowered Liza to the dark hole in the basin, ready to drop her in.

Griffin's eyelids were shut tight, but he couldn't block the ruby Glare. He saw red. Suffering was the only sensation his body could register, and red was the only color in the universe.

Griffin had launched his small body at his giant dad, who had held out a hand to stop the weak missile. Instead of slamming into him pointlessly, Griffin had pulled up and bit his dad's vulnerable, outstretched hand. Hard. His dad had yelled, trying to simultaneously pull his hand out of his son's mouth and drop the lizard into the garbage disposal. The anole's tail snapped off, swinging the lizard to the counter beside the basin instead of straight down into the hole of the garbage disposal. Liza scurried off in a scribble of green. Griffin would find the dried brown husk of her tailless body in the bottom cabinet a week later.

Griffin couldn't drop body parts to escape, and his dad had grabbed his skinny arm with one fleshy fist while bringing his other fist down hard to connect with Griffin's chin. Griffin's head had snapped back for a dimming view

238

of the light fixture in the middle of the ceiling and then he hit the back of his head on the edge of the table. Everything had gone black.

Here, everything was red. Everything was pain. His chest was like the Opened Ones. He was crushed under the foot of a diamond giant. He was dissolved in a tree made of cages. He was a playground for pain.

He had awoken in the hospital, but immediately pretended that he was still unconscious. He always did that when dad hit him too hard. He'd never ended up in the hospital, though. Usually it was his own bed. He had heard his mom talking, but it took a few seconds to realize she was lying to a doctor or a nurse about what had happened to him. Protecting his dad.

They had taken him in for a head scan to see if he had any long black fractures in the glowing white of his skull. He was fine, a doctor had said. The biggest misdiagnosis in the entire history of medicine. On the way home, his mom promised him a new lizard and all the fast food he could eat. And when they arrived, they found that his dad had disappeared, all his stuff gone. All that was left of him as a reminder was a dead lizard and the bruises on Griffin's jaw.

CHAPTER 42

Hit It All Very Hard

Instant relief from the past. Instant relief from the present. Griffin wondered, as he lay on the cool metal floor on the far side of the Glare, feeling like a piece of burning iron thrust into a bucket of ice water, if maybe, maybe the whole fascination that the Merciless had with the Glare was how they felt after passing through it. He laughed at the thought of Gutter going through the glowing red door of its house and then lying down on its back with its metal-tipped hands behind its white boulder of a head and sighing in relief through its pointy metal teeth.

And then he realized that all this thinking and laughing meant that he was still alive. Sweaty and aching and trembling, and too close to memories that should have been farther away, but alive. Alive, alive, alive.

He had survived an intensity of Glare that nobody, not

even near-immortal creatures made of rock and metal, had survived before.

A sensation in his fist caught his attention, mostly out of surprise that he could feel anything after the pain of the Glare. He opened it to see a bright fragment of his yellow cast, one that he had saved during his loneliness in the cell after discarding the rest. Laila's name was shouting at him from the bright yellow. He had held on to it in the Glare.

And that reminded him he needed to save his best friend and his bully and everybody else at Osshua Elementary.

The hallway was metal and black like everything else in the Forge and this world, and he suddenly loved the aesthetic. He stuck the fragment of cast into a pocket of his shredded pants and flailed down the hall like a Jesus Christ lizard to the small room that was the cortex for the entire Forge.

Inside the room, everything was covered in Black Slide hide, just like in the control center. The walls, the ceiling, the floor, all the control consoles that filled the small space. If Griffin's eyes had been metal cones, maybe he would have seen all the invisible controls. Maybe he would have seen enough to understand how to reset the Glare on his own. He couldn't see anything but a black room, though.

Fortunately, he didn't need to see anything but a black room.

He reached to his belt loop and slid out a spiked black cudgel. Gutter had given it to him with extremely precise instructions. "Hit everything in that room until the Glare shuts down," it had said. "Hit it all very hard."

And that's exactly what Griffin Birch did.

Instead of eye-cones and metal-tipped fingers skillfully poking and scraping the controls, Griffin had the metal spikes of a cudgel and simple blunt force. He wielded that cudgel like the clubs of the cavemen he had seen in cartoons, like the broadswords of the knights in the movies, like the staffs of the martial artists in video games. He smashed panel after panel, and it felt good. He smashed Leech and Gutter and every Merciless he had met. He smashed Diants and mound monsters and squid stones. He hacked down cage trees with mighty blows of his ax. He destroyed the Torture Dungeon and the painground and the Forge and the Painful Place. He smashed his dad's face repeatedly. He broke the Black Slide into small bits.

A random scrape of spike conjured a set of screens on the wall. One showed a flood of Merciless pouring through the entrance to the Forge. Another showed a Diant kicking over a train like it was a toy in a nursery. Another showed a painground full of torture devices and his classmates.

Griffin doubled his efforts, tripled them, quadrupled,

feeling the vibrations of his violence all the way to his shoulders, the shock of his blows in the back of his skull, the sweat dripping down his face and arms and legs.

The entire time, the small ruby-red glow at the end of the hall stuck in his sight like a flaw in his iris, like the lit end of one of his dad's cigarettes. As much as he tried to get lost in the violence of his task, he couldn't forget the Glare. Still, he was a drummer, a lumberjack, a railroad worker; he was winning all the tests of strength in all the carnivals that ever stretched out their tents under an autumn sky.

It felt both good and bad, both a release and a frustration. Despite his violence, the dull black material was as undamaged, as untouched as the black sky of the Painful Place. Like he was a weakling, unable so much as to scratch or dent the surfaces. He had no idea if he was succeeding or failing.

And then the deep red winked out. His eye was healed. The cigarette doused. The hallway open. He had beaten the Glare into submission. Maybe everything into submission.

CHAPTER 43

We're in Trouble

Griffin hadn't taken two steps out of the cortex when a nightmare of Merciless rushed at him down the corridor. He changed his stance and held his cudgel in front of him, knowing even as he did so that a skinny kid in lizard underwear wasn't exactly threatening. But that didn't matter. Even if he'd had somewhere to run and hide, he wouldn't have gone. Not this time. But as the stone and metal creatures parted around him, he realized they were wearing the vertical strips of the Forge Merciless. They swarmed through the cortex, scrabbling at the panels with their eyes and hands almost more viciously than he had been able to do with a weapon.

Griffin hadn't taken two more steps out of the cortex when he was rushed by Laila and Ozzie. They collided in the corridor, a hysterical, joyful ball of soft arms and soft legs and soft chests, warm bodies and wide smiles, soft eyes full of soft tears.

"Way to go, Griffin!" said Ozzie, pronouncing his name like he used to.

"You did it!" said Laila.

Griffin reached into his pocket and showed her the fragment of cast. She gave him another hug.

"Is it over?" Griffin asked. "I saw Opened Ones get into the building."

"Not yet," said Ozzie. "But the second the Glare turned off, every Merciless started fighting to the death with their control panels. They're trying to get the Glare for the whole Forge going again."

They exited the corridor to a panicked ant farm of black-clad Merciless dashing across the control center to various screens and panels. Gutter stood on the dais scratching at consoles and screech-grumbling orders. Somehow, Griffin felt like he was on the deck of an old ship in the middle of a stormy sea and everyone on board was working desperately to keep it from capsizing.

A cluster of screens on one wall showed the reason for the commotion and mirrored what Griffin had seen in the cortex. Opened Ones clogged entire corridors of the Forge while brandishing cudgels, shields, and Glare weapons. They fought the Forge Merciless on the painground, a battle that was a macrocosm of the one they had witnessed in the control center, except instead of three kids watching from the ceiling, it was now scores of kids watching in horror, confusion, and hope, while strapped to painground equipment.

Outside, the Diants surrounded the Forge and battled a fleet of tanklike black vehicles that must have come either from one of the outbuildings or from the city. Although battle was the wrong word. It was more like the Diants were fighting a swarm of ground beetles, smashing the black tanks with one stomp of their diamond feet.

Griffin and Laila and Ozzie tried to stay out of the way of the Merciless in the control center. There was nothing for them to do. They stuck close to one of the walls. Behind them on a screen, the squid stone kept blinking.

"I guess we know who to root for now," said Ozzie.

"Yeah," said Griffin. Their only way to escape the Painful Place and protect their home was for Gutter and the Forge Merciless to get the Glare turned back on to repel the invading Opened Ones. He was rooting for the Merciless. He was rooting for the Forge. He was rooting for the Glare. Things had changed so much.

And then they changed again.

The Opened Ones breached the control room. They poured in from both doorways like an oil spill, weapons ready and teeth bared in metal snarls. Forge Merciless quickly attempted to fend them off, and soon the nightmare of Merciless was a chaos of them.

This time, there was no way for Griffin, Laila, and Ozzie to make it to the safety of the ceiling guts. They were trapped in the middle of a brutal battle of sizzling red Glare and thudding black cudgels.

"We're in trouble," said Ozzie. He held the hand Glare in front of him, and it hummed loudly as he swung the disc randomly, like he was holding a drone with a mind of its own.

"The cells!" said Griffin. It was the only hiding place in the entire control room.

They jumped into separate cells, pulling the doors toward them, but not shutting them all the way, not wanting to get trapped inside. It reminded Griffin of his first time in a cell, when it dropped to the floor and the door broke. He just needed to have Laila's knee in his ribs and her elbow in his neck. How long ago was that? A day? A week? Six months? A whole different Griffin ago?

The fight was feral and ferocious and, like everything the Merciless did, seemed undertaken with a violent glee. The violence was far worse to watch at eye level than it had been from the ceiling. In the ceiling, far above, Griffin had felt detached, like seeing a bustling city from an airplane.

But down here, with the dust of battered heads slinging through the bars to sting his eyes and grit his teeth, it was more real. More terrifying.

Griffin jammed his face against the bars to get a wider view of the fight. It was impossible to tell whether the Forge Merciless were winning. But a lot of individual Merciless were losing. Their small, monstrous bodies lay about the dull black floor of the control room, chunks of their heads missing. Others ran around holding their heads in agony, scarred by their metal headdresses being ripped out of their skulls. Griffin looked for the only Merciless he knew and quickly found him. Gutter was playing king of the mountain on the raised dais, shooting a Glare weapon with one hand at any Opened One who got close while gouging at the control panel in front of it with its other.

Until a flash of red surrounded it, and Gutter fell to the floor grabbing at its torso.

A Merciless in a sash stepped onto the dais. It had a metal bar like a snorkel extending up the side of its head and a cudgel raised in its fist to pulverize Gutter.

Griffin's cell was suddenly empty, the door swinging wildly open to bang on its hinges.

CHAPTER 44

Not All Soft Children Will Survive

Griffin was the comet this time. His feet were fire and his body ice and rock. But he remembered Laila bouncing off the Merciless she had attacked when they rescued Ozzie, so he didn't throw himself squarely at Snorkel Head. He threw himself at the back of Snorkel Head's knees.

Griffin hit them just as the cudgel dropped. Snorkel Head's joints caved, and it fell backward over Griffin, a grinding shriek erupting from its black mouth. Griffin recovered from the collision quickly but stayed low on the dais beside Gutter's unconscious form, not wanting to attract eye-cones. He saw Snorkel Head stand up, and it directed its own eye-cones at Griffin like it wanted to fire them at him from its sockets. The Opened One had hung on to its cudgel in the fall, and it raised the weapon as it charged at Griffin.

Griffin threw his arms over his head at the last second,

and felt the cudgel connect with his weak arm. He felt the spikes open his flesh, heard the crunch of his bone. His arm flopped out of his control, but he didn't feel pain. He tried to keep protecting his head with his other arm and heard another crunch. He wiggled the fingers on his good arm and realized the crunch wasn't his bone this time. He looked and saw Snorkel Head reeling backward, its snorkel bent sideways and a crack in its white head. The Merciless screeched and fell to the ground. Griffin turned away when he saw the boot come down on its head. Gutter's boot. He heard the sound, though.

"Soft child." Griffin looked up to see the Merciless throw down a cudgel, which hit the dais in a puff of white dust. Gutter returned to the control panel, but kept its eye-cones trained on Griffin like there weren't a million more important things to look at in the control center. Griffin cradled his rubbery arm that still didn't hurt. He kept waiting for the pain to come. Gutter licked its pointy teeth with its black tongue. It lifted its fingers, tight together in almost a salute, and then jabbed them into the control panel.

Everything went red.

Griffin squeezed his eyes shut and winced, heard the thunder of an army of bodies striking the floor and the metal-rock screams of Merciless in agony. He felt a body fall on him.

But, like with his broken arm, Griffin barely felt the Glare. It might as well have been hot light. He opened his eyes and saw that the control center was carpeted with fallen bodies, both Opened Ones and Forge Merciless. None of them moved. None of them made a sound. Even the screens on the wall were still and silent. It was like the entire room was freeze-framed. Like Griffin had gotten stuck in a moment of time.

And then that moment was over. A grinding of rock and shearing of metal made him turn his head. Gutter was up, scraping its eyes across a console, and other Merciless were stirring. Not all of them, though. Screens on the wall showed the aftermath of the Glare. It was the control room times a thousand, the bodies of Merciless strewn across metal floor. Outside, among the shredded carapaces of the black tank vehicles, the Diants ambled away like they'd grown bored with the destruction.

"The high-intensity Glare must have desensitized you to pain. That is too bad," said Gutter, watching Griffin like it was waiting for something from him. It apparently didn't get it, though, because it changed the subject. "The Glare destroyed all the Opened Ones. And some of the Forge Merciless. My control of the Glare was not complete yet, but I couldn't wait for it to be. It was more power-ful than I intended." And then Gutter said something that seemed more to himself than to Griffin. "I think that not all soft children will survive."

"Laila!" Griffin hadn't felt the pain of his arm breaking or the pain of the Glare. But he felt this pain. It shot up his chest like a rapidly growing tree, its pointy branches stabbing his insides and filling his throat. He jumped off the dais and ran toward the cells. He saw her limp on the floor. His stomach turned heavy, full of stone.

"Laila!" Griffin knelt and tried to shake her awake, but she didn't respond. He bent his ear to her chest and, after holding his breath for what seemed like an hour, heard the beat of her heart. And then he heard her groan.

"I . . . hate . . . the . . . Glare." Laila's eyes fluttered like the dark room was too bright and then she stared at the ceiling for a few moments. Griffin helped her sit up. "Griffin, your arm! What happened to it?"

Griffin looked down and saw it covered in red and bent sickeningly. "What do you mean?" he joked.

"It looks bad," said Laila. "We need to get you help." She tore her eyes from Griffin's mangled arm. "Where's Ozzie?"

"There is no Ozzie," said a familiar voice behind them. "Only a massive headache stuffed inside a soft child." Ozzie was sitting on the floor closer to the cells with his head between his knees, rubbing at his temples. "I don't ever want to even see the color red again."

The Forge rumbled, and all three looked at the

schematic of the Black Slide on the wall. It didn't seem to be registering any change. "Is the Black Tunnel still growing?" asked Griffin, but neither Laila nor Ozzie answered because they couldn't hear him. The Forge kept rumbling and wouldn't stop. A cell dropped from the ceiling track to the floor with a crash.

They got up and tried to run for a door, but the shaking of the Forge, and all the Merciless bodies scattered across the floor, made it hard. They only made it as far as the dais, where Gutter was scraping its eye-cones so hard across a control panel it looked like he was trying to rub them off. It looked up and bared its metal teeth at Griffin in that way that the Merciless used to mean everything from *Hello* to *I want to hurt you.*

And then the Forge was still. A single piece of the ceiling guts fell, adding an exclamation point to the violence. Griffin looked over at the wall, but the schematic of the Black Slide had disappeared.

"What happened?" asked Griffin.

"The Black Slide has been restored," said Gutter.

"Yes! We're going home!" said Ozzie.

Laila tried to hug Griffin, but then backed off when she saw his arm again. Griffin shrugged, a smile on his face.

"No," said Gutter. It was the ugliest sound Griffin had ever heard from a Merciless. His smile disappeared.

"What do you mean, no?" asked Laila.

"The experiments must continue," said Gutter.

Griffin leaped to the dais, his bad arm bumping useless at his side. He got so close to Gutter he almost skewered his eyes on the eye-cones of the Merciless. "You promised you'd send us all home."

Gutter didn't respond.

"You promised," Griffin repeated slowly.

"He saved your life from Snorkel Head," said Ozzie. "And your Forge."

"He saved your chance at immortality," said Laila.

Gutter and Griffin continued to stare at each other, each stony, each waiting for the other to back down.

Finally, Gutter's boulder of a head cracked into a feral grin. "I will send you all home. We cannot finish the experiments anyway. This Forge has been compromised."

Griffin relaxed, stepping back and rubbing at his numb, broken arm.

"Wait. You couldn't continue the experiments anyway? Were you joking, then?" asked Ozzie. "Do Merciless joke?"

"I just wanted to do one more small experiment." Gutter ran its tiny black tongue over its metal teeth as it aimed its eye-cones at Griffin. "On the soft child who entered the Black Slide twice."

CHAPTER 45

Do You Still Love Reptiles?

Griffin landed roughly on the red mulch of the Osshua Elementary School playground in a puff of cold air. He felt the shift immediately and turned around. The Black Slide was gone, replaced by the original plastic orange slide.

His mom was there somehow, and she took him in her arms, crying about his torn clothes and the blood and his floppy arm that still didn't hurt. He looked down at himself in the warm sunlight. He did look like he'd stomped repeatedly by a Diant.

He was the last one through, and he found himself exchanging the chaos of a battle for the chaos of a media event. It took a few days for him and Laila and Ozzie to piece everything together.

The fifth graders of Osshua Elementary had returned over the course of a day, appearing sporadically at the

255

bottom of the Black Slide like gumballs from a gumball machine. The anesthetized area that Leech had mentioned must have worn off—once the children started appearing, all the adults were waiting there like it was school pickup.

The kids had been gone for only a week on this side of the slide, and despite what Gutter had said, everybody had survived that final Glare. They were apparently harder than it thought.

Kids were whisked away to homes and given warm dinners and fretted over and tucked in. Griffin's mom acted like she had awakened from a sleepwalk she had been doing since his dad had left. Maybe even since before that. She took him to the doctor, had his wounds tended, his arm wrapped in a cast—a cast that this time was a beautiful vine-snake green that he didn't let Laila get anywhere near with a permanent marker.

But the truth of what had happened to the fifth graders of Osshua Elementary School never came out.

While everybody had survived the Glare, only Griffin, Laila, and Ozzie remembered the Painful Place. And everyone else seemed different. Older. Like the rest of the fifth graders had been through more summer breaks than Griffin and Laila and Ozzie. At first, they tried to discuss the Painful Place with their classmates, but they were made fun of. They were told to stop being babies, to stop playing pretend

256

games, making up imaginary worlds. They were laughed at for being kids who watched too many cartoons. The three learned fast to keep the Painful Place to themselves.

The adults' recollection of the whole thing was so blurry and vague it might as well not have happened. In the end, they treated it like a bad field trip or a bus accident, and everybody was just grateful that the kids were back and safe, and they moved on with their lives.

The rest of fifth-grade year was . . . boring. Pleasantly boring. The Torture Chamber didn't seem at all like one anymore. Mrs. Pitts was barely intimidating despite her lighthouse height. Nobody stared out the windows at the playground anymore.

Eventually, Griffin and Laila and Ozzie started feeling the effects of their time in the Painful Place as well. Like the experiments had accelerated their hardening. Or maybe they were just growing up. Ozzie seemed to feel it the most. By the end of fifth grade, he had drifted from Griffin and Laila. He hung out mostly with Desda, which Griffin and Laila were happy to see.

Laila and Griffin made a pact: they wouldn't let the world harden them, no matter what happened. They didn't want to become like the Merciless. Or like most adults. They focused on their passions. Griffin spent his time convincing his mother to get him an iguana, which he eventually got. He turned an entire spare room into its habitat. He named it Liza.

Laila kept looking at the stars, got a new telescope to add to her corral, and convinced her mom to take her to Mexico that summer to see the Large Millimeter Telescope, one of the most cutting-edge observatories in the world. Griffin went with them. Mexico is second only to Australia for having the most reptile species on the planet.

Griffin never fully got his sense of pain back. Sometimes that was an amazing superpower. More often, it was extremely dangerous. Like when he touched a hot stove without realizing it and only knew something bad was happening to him when he smelled burnt meat. And anytime he tripped he had to make sure nothing was broken because he wouldn't know otherwise.

Sixth grade happened. Seventh grade. Eighth. In ninth grade, Griffin's mother fell in love with someone she met on a dating app, who lived far away in Arizona. They would fly back and forth to see each other, but soon made the decision that Griffin and his mom would move out there. At least Arizona had great reptiles. Laila and Griffin kept in touch online. They went to different colleges. They both got married, had kids. Griffin had a girl named Meredith. Laila, a boy named Claude.

Once a month, without fail, they would call each

other. And although Laila never became an astronaut and Griffin never became a herpetologist, Laila would ask Griffin, "Do you still love reptiles? Do you dream about feeding hunks of meat to crocodiles?" And Griffin would say, "Yes, I do. This month I went to the zoo to see the tuataras." Or "This month I watched a documentary about flying snakes." And then he would ask Laila, "What about you? Do you still love the stars? Do you dream about making footprints on Mars?" And Laila would say, "Yes, I do. This month I lay down on a blanket in my backyard and watched the Perseid meteor shower." Or "This month I read a science-fiction novel."

And then they would ask about each other's children. Laila would ask about Meredith. "Does she still love archaeology? Does she dream of digging up pieces of pottery?" And Griffin would say, "Yes, she does. This month we went to an Egyptian exhibit at the history museum." And then Griffin would ask about Claude. "Does he still like to bake? Does he dream of making the world's largest cake?" And Laila would say, "Yes, he does. This month he made brownies for the school bake sale."

And that's as close as they got to talking about the Merciless or the Painful Place.

And they might have fallen out of touch eventually— except one day, Laila dropped Claude off at her ex-husband's house and saw in the backyard the Christmas present he had given their son. It was a playground set with a couple of swings and a climbing wall and, in the middle of the setup, much too large for it, a Black Slide.

ACKNOWLEDGMENTS

The designation "author" contains multitudes. In my case, it includes my wife, Lindsey, and daughters, Esme, Hazel, and Olive, for being continual sources of inspiration for me and for putting up with a husband and father who's continuously living in two worlds at once. It includes my agent, Alex Slater, who somehow fully supported *"Hellraiser* for kids" as a concept and has become an important part of my life and invaluable to my work. It includes Christian Haunton and Adam Perry, for trudging through an even bleaker version of the book than the one you now hold and who helped me polish the Painful Place to a dull shine.

It includes Elizabeth Lynch at Harper, both for being the reason I get to acknowledge everyone here, but even more for not balking at the book I really wanted to write. Also for putting together such an ace book team—Maya Myers on copyedits, Jeannette Arroyo, Catherine Lee, and Jessie Gang, for the remarkable cover that really belongs on a classic children's book instead of one of mine.

The journey down the Black Slide is a lot easier when you're not alone.